1

Beauty Scars

Kern Carter

ISBN: 1546875549
ISBN 13: 9781546875543
Library of Congress Control Number: **XXXXX (If applicable)**
LCCN Imprint Name: **City and State (If applicable)**

Foreword

"Beauty - be not caused - It is."

- Emily Dickinson (1830-1886)

Beauty is everywhere. Even when all hope seems lost. Though it may feel hidden, it's there. Beauty is everywhere.

If in darkness, and for a moment you feel blind, simply listen and hear it whisper on the wind. If for a moment you feel deaf, simply smell the aroma in the air. If you cannot, simply taste it on your tongue. If nothing still, just breathe. Feel the air pass through your lungs. Feel the rush of blood in your veins and the beating of your own heart. Feel the shock of neural electricity coursing through your nerves enlightening your brain.

And know if you ever forget or ever believe that there is no more beauty left in the world, simply remember that beauty is found beyond all that you can see, hear, smell, taste or touch. Beauty is far more sensual than that. Beauty is the fire that burns eternally in our souls and is reflected in every soul we encounter. Be it human, creature, plant or amoeba. Be it vapour, liquid, or solid mass. Be it flesh or stone. Beauty is within and without. Beauty seeks Truth. Truth is Beauty. Perhaps, that is the only answer we need.

Kern has discovered this truth in Treasure and Justin. Two souls searching, hiding, battling, surrendering. To truth and beauty, like children wanting to be seen and heard, wanting to be understood behind all the masks, wanting to be respected, honoured and forgiven. Beneath every scar, they find beauty through love. Beauty through fear. The fear of actually being seen and heard. Of actually having love returned.

Through them, Kern has given us an empathic mirror into our own souls. An example of how we can own our own scars. How truth can unveil our beauty, though it be hidden behind every shadow of a doubt. Their story reveals that the way out can be found within. That the way out is through. We just need to choose to go forward. Turn the page. Go forward. Let your Beauty Scars shine.

- Shomee Chakrabartty

4

VOL i

TREASURE

An accident made me beautiful.

I sat in the passenger seat of our dirt coloured two-door staring through rolled up windows. My mother chased my father and the stranger outside the bar. She screamed. When that didn't work, she screamed some more, pleading for my father to stop.

The stranger made it to her knees before my father pushed her back down. She fought to her knees again and faced my dad. It was only then he caught a glimpse of me, both our eyes frozen.

Then I ran. I opened the door and ran towards my father into the flailing snow that covered the sidewalks. My mom's screams. Different this time. Not for mercy but screams of horror as my body rolled violently across the street.

I became beautiful by accident, and to this day I'm not sure I would ever take that back. For me, that accident is the second most important day of my life, the first being my birth, another dubious tale if you listen to my mother tell it. And she did tell it. Over and over again, any chance she got.

You could almost feel it coming.

"Tommy tried everything to get that car started," she'd begin. "And you know he's no stranger to an engine and some tools. But you know how these winters get...and even if Tommy did get that car started, I doubt we would've made it ten yards down our block."

At least I knew that part of the story was true. Winter in Valleyfield was furious, never-ending snowfalls and cascades of ice. It held the town hostage. No one in, no one out.

"I knew I was about to have my baby right inside that car. Tommy finally realized it too, and ran back inside the house to grab whatever blankets he could fit in both arms."

This is inevitably where everyone hearing the story for the first time would ask the obvious: "Why didn't Tommy just bring you inside?"

Dad never answered this question. In fact, he was hardly ever around when my mom told the story, which is odd because she told it so much.

"Well that's just not important, dear." Or "I was making such a fuss he must have thought why bother. I mean, what difference would it have made? It was just as cold inside that damn house."

My mom just wanted to get to her favourite part. And I know I should be way more proud that she made up a half bullshit story to prove how special I was, a story she must have fully believed herself by now. But I really never cared about how I was born, or how my mother told everyone I was born. My life started after that accident.

"The frost," my mom would power on, "was all I could see on the windows when I pushed my baby out. Then I saw those eyes. Those eyes sparkling green as ancient emeralds." Then my favourite part of the entire tale and the only part I didn't mind hearing:

"I knew right then she was a gift to be treasured, so that's what I named her."

Treasure. My saving grace. A name that actually means something, that actually makes me feel something.

The only thing till that accident.

My mother sat beside me in that green chair with metal legs every single night I was in the hospital and we counted my beauty marks one by one out loud.

"One beauty mark, two beauty marks, three beauty marks…"

On and on we went, discovering new ones before I closed my eyes each night. Mom told me this mythical tale about how new beauty marks started growing while I slept and that I would have to wake up every morning if I wanted them to finish growing. Ridiculous, but I believed her, and kept waking up, and they kept growing. We added them to our count each night and giggled like two school friends texting at the back of the classroom.

"You keep those emeralds open, sweety. They're your treasure."

Yes, yes, they are. A lost Treasure finally found. And now they aren't fighting against a head stuck staring at the ground, or cheeks that squinted my emeralds into non-existence. They're here, right here for everyone to see, and stare, and to comment on how they sparkled even within the eeriness of hospital walls.

Could you imagine?

My life before this was as dim as my father's eyes. I had to insert all the colour myself.

And I hated writing so I never kept a journal. But I was eight when I got my first cell phone and the voice recorder was everything for me. I'd always volunteer to walk to the convenience store when my mom was cooking. Or on days mom had to stay late after school, I'd walk the half a mile home with the phone to my ear like I was really talking to someone.

But I wasn't. Just me, just my thoughts out loud. I think about how much of my life was on that phone. How much I shared without reservation. It's amazing what you say when no one's listening. Makes you realize how much of your actual thoughts you hold back in real conversation.

I told that phone everything, though. Just really short streams of thought that I thought only made sense to me.

"Daddy was up really late last night. He sounded like he had a cold again. Mommy was snoring. Three teachers called her beautiful at school today. Seven teachers called Mommy beautiful at school yesterday. I think it's because her hair looks better when it's down. Mommy never wears her hair down but Daddy's hair is always down. I wonder if Daddy will be up late again tonight. If he'll come get me from my room so we can look at the watchtowers."

Back under the beeps. I can hear the slow drips of whatever's in that bag injected into my arm. This room smells like iron and metal and blood. I know where I am, just as consciously as I know when I start dreaming. There he is, sitting on a bench at the tip of the lake, his feet drawing patterns in the sand. He turns around to see me walking behind him. His smile. My eyes. Now we sit on the bench together.

"Are you dreaming?" he asks.

"Are you dreaming?" I ask. Neither of us answers. I tell him about watchtowers, he tells me about skyscrapers. We talk and keep talking. But then it's time to go, we both feel it.

"Till we dream again..."

***

*One beauty mark, two beauty marks, three beauty marks...*My mom is counting my beauty marks again, this time in the morning while I'm still half asleep. I hear the doctor and her mumble about having too many.

"It's because I'm beautiful," I try to say. My mom strokes my hair and tells me to shut my eyes. They both step outside to continue whispering. I don't feel so good that morning. My head is spinning more than usual. I open my eyes again and there's Dad, sitting in his wheelchair.

The cost of my beauty staring right at me.

I jump out of the bed and grab his face. He's smiling but not the smile I'm used to. The tragedy in his eyes is different.

"How you feeling this morning, Treasure?"

"I'm fine, Daddy. I feel better."

He smiles again. The tragedy is different and something darker has taken its place. I can't describe it yet, but I know it's there. It's staring right at me, always staring like it can't believe, or wants to believe but doesn't know how.

"I'm really OK, Daddy. Doctors say I'll be out of here soon."

"I almost killed you." He can't control his tears.

"But you didn't, Daddy. You didn't kill me. You saved me; you saved me and I'm fine."

The crowns of our heads join.

"When you getting out of this thing, Daddy? When you gonna be able to walk again?"

He wipes his face with the heel of his hand, still speaking deliberately. "Maybe a year, maybe longer, maybe not that long. They don't know. Depends on rehab and some other stuff."

We sat still for a bit till Mom came through the door, minus her whisper buddy.

"Brought you both something to eat, seeing how neither of you are eating the crap they're serving in here."

My mother. Caring, sensitive, protective, but beautiful. To the last point she seems oblivious, like she really doesn't know. Maybe she doesn't, or maybe she really just doesn't care. But how is that possible?

How can she not? My mother can wake up, splash water on her face, put her hair up and be splendid. She knows that. She has to, right? But nothing about her ever felt gilded. She spoke with confidence without condescending, and shared intimate parts of herself with everyone she met.

No temptation, no provoking, no miscommunications. Judging her by stares alone would put her in a box. It wasn't till meeting her that you knew.

But I knew, and I still couldn't believe.

ALL THAT POWER.

I remember being a little girl and sneaking into her room on Sunday mornings. Daddy was already up and out. She would be propped up on three pillows reading whatever she was reading.

"I see you," she'd say. And I'd jump onto the bed and slide under the covers right next to her. She would smile, take me under one arm and keep reading. I would just stare at her. My mother. Her eyelashes that curled only at the edges. The way both her lips moved just a little as she mouthed each sentence. Her skin a shade lighter than mine and without any of the freckles that plagued my own.

My mother. With cheeks like a six-month-old baby and just as soft. How can she not know, or not care? She let me play with her hair while she read. Sometimes I would fall asleep again, almost hypnotized by my gazing. I'd wake up and she'd still be there.

***

I actually wish I could tell you my dad is an alcoholic, then I'd fit in better with more of the troubled kids at school. But my dad is a drug addict, mostly cocaine, but he dabbles in anything he can snort up his nose.

And addict is my word; my way of describing my father. He would argue that since his veins are clean and his family is still in tact that he couldn't possibly have a serious problem. But 'serious' is such a bullshit word. Falling asleep 30 seconds after putting your five-year-old daughter on your back to play horse is something I'd call serious. Waking your six-year-old daughter at three in the morning on a school night to look at the stars is something I'd call serious.

But that's Daddy. Tommy, the hero, my hero, the one who made me beautiful. The scapegoat, the tip of the index, mover of everything according to all these school counsellors. It's strange that I can't remember what I wore two weeks ago but can relive moments with my dad when I was just five and six years old.

"Look at all those pretty stars, Treasure. Shining bright like your eyes on the day you were born."

My dad's own eyes are dim, and he has this way of looking at you that feels like tragedy happening over and over and over again.

"I think the stars are like eyes, sweety. All of them staring down at us every night like endless rows of watchtowers."

"What's a watchtower?"

"A watchtower is a tall building with a big light that watches over the water and keeps everyone safe."

"So, stars keep everyone safe?"

"Stars make sure everyone follows their dreams, Treasure. What's your dream? What do you want to be more than anything when you grow up?"

"I want to be a star."

Recording:

BEAUTY IS POWER. did that work? Wait.

BEAUTY IS POWER.

BEAUTY IS POWER. There we go.

What is it that thing that Mommy has? What is it? How does she get all that attention? She doesn't even try. She doesn't even care. But she gets it, all of it. She gets other teachers to drive her home when Daddy works late. She gets all the teachers to stare at her when she walks through the hallways.

BEAUTY IS POWER.

And she didn't give me any of it. Boys don't offer me their snacks like they do to Amanda. Boys don't fight over me at recess like they do to Amanda. I'm just here to be friends with the girl who gets all the attention. My mom the teacher who gets all the attention. One day, I'll shine. Bright as watchtowers. Bright as my mother in the hallways.

Pause. Save. Rename. Beauty24.

Trapped again. Trapped like Amy Dunne minus all the crazy shit, just the part where she felt forced to live in Carthage and reminisced about her past life in New York City. Toronto is my New York, except that it's my future not my past. The place me and my friends make up stories about and listen to our parents chastise and pretend their lives are better off far away from the city.

"Eaton's Centre is the size of all of Valleyfield."

"Celebrities actually go to their clubs."

"They actually have clubs."

"Only parents and deer like Valleyfield."

But now. This accident. Now I get it. Now I see it; now they see me.

God, it feels so good to look this goddamn good.

I just say that out loud sometimes. To myself, in my room, or the bathroom after I shower and the mirror is all steamed up. I'm just happy, you know. Just really happy with the way I look. How many girls can say that and actually mean it?

I mean really mean it. Not try to convince themselves or pretend to mean it. Like actually wake up in the morning, look at themselves in the mirror and say, "I love the way I look."

The accident made me this way. It happened at the tail end of winter and by the time I got out and was actually able to do anything, it was weeks into the summer. Me and my mom spent the rest of the time up at our cottage in Kincardine. Dad only came once, I think, not wanting to spoil the party, he said, but we all knew why he chose to stay away. Mom was a school teacher, though, so she had plenty of time. We wasted all of it on Lake Huron, tubing, drinking beers on the beach (mom let me have one a day), doing a lot of nothing.

Except dreaming...

The same dream. No, not the same dream, but the same boy. I can tell he's the same even though I can't tell what he looks like. I know his face. I see the scar under his chin, I hear the politeness in his voice. I hear it because I think it's strange for someone my age to have that quality.

"You again," I say.

"Me again."

"Do you remember me?"

"I remember you. Do you remember me?"

"Of course," I say. Each word brings us a step closer. Each step drifts us further apart. He holds out his hand and I take it. Everything stops now. We're together, sitting with nothing or no one around us.

"Where are you?" he asks.

"I'm right here."

"No, I mean, where are you?"

I smile, then open my eyes.

***

The better I started feeling, the more I ventured out on my own around Kincardine.

"Just keep your cell close by," is what my mom said every time I left right after morning tea and a full plate of turkey bacon and eggs, or blueberry pancakes with honey instead of maple syrup. She stood at the door and watched me till I disappeared. I could feel her stare, and sometimes I looked back and waved another 'see you later.'

"I stood at that door for at least ten minutes," she told me on one of our drives back to Valleyfield. "I hoped you'd forget something and come running back. Or just change your mind and want to stay with me."

"What'd you think I was doing?"

"Exactly what a teenager would be doing."

That was an abrupt end to our conversation. I didn't exactly know what she meant but was pretty sure it had something to do with something I didn't want to talk about. Who talks about that kind of stuff with their parents--crushes and kisses and too much hormones?

I'd say my first kiss was the latter. A meagre looking blond haired boy named Ben who lived a few doors down. He looked like he needed me as much as I needed him. And when we both ended up in my backyard with my mom at the grocery store and my dad still at the group home. We made out till we heard the car pull up to the driveway.

Before that I grabbed his hand and pushed it down my pants. He didn't even know what to do. I still held it there, though. The pressure was enough, and eventually he snuck his fingers inside. Neither of us ever told anyone. We were both too embarrassed. Me of him and vice versa. Ben ended up moving away before we started high school. A small relief.

But that summer in Kincardine I was tame. I didn't know yet. Not quite. Everything was still so new. When Dad came up that one weekend, I didn't go anywhere on my own. We spent both days together driving in and out of town, climbing through paths that forced us to wear shoes, barbecuing on the deck and watching mom do yoga on the beach.

"How you feeling, Treasure?"

"Good, Daddy. Feeling pretty good."

"Your mom says you been heading out a lot during the day. Just getting some space?"

"You could say that. I mean, I'm not coming back home too much past dark. I'm just exploring Daddy, that's all."

I saw something in the way my dad looked at me just then. It wasn't fear or any kind of judgement or anything like that. He was just painfully accepting that I was growing up.

"Don't worry, Daddy. I'm still your Treasure. That's never gonna change."

***

Lanterns. Red lanterns. That was the first time I crossed the line that summer. My exploration walks were really just me hanging out with my friend Jody and her boyfriend, Jake. We'd do the same thing me and my mom did except Jody wasn't my mom. Her cousin Drew came up for the last couple weeks I was there. He'd always hover a little too close, or rush to beat Jake to building the beach fire. He was cute, nothing special, but I'll never forget him because he was how I knew for sure.

Jake and I were fixing up lanterns with Jody chatting with Drew in the sand. It was already dark enough to see all the constellations and shooting stars over the lake.

"We need some kindling, Jody. Why don't you and Drew run go grab some and let me and Treasure finish with these lanterns."

"You mean walk over to the other side of the beach?" Jody wasn't feeling adventurous.

"Why would I even ask? Come on, Treasure. Can you two at least handle these lanterns?"

There's an energy between boys and girls. Something that happens when two people who are attracted to each other end up alone. And there are very few things that can match this energy - good intentions, will power - everything seems weakened every second you're in each other's presence.

Then excitement, like thrill excitement. That alone can make you drip. That's more powerful than any kind of moral whatever you think you can hold on to. In the end, it's only those moments that matter.

When we came back half an hour later walking way too far apart, Jody and Drew knew. Drew wasn't so quick to fix the flames after that, and did everything but curl his tail under his ass. He didn't speak to me for two days till I texted him to come over to my cottage for dinner. I held his hand and walked him inside, played with his feet under the table while we ate, and lay down across his lap for half a movie before falling asleep. I woke up to him stroking my hair.

That's the first time I knew.

Whispers, whispers, whispers. No one trusts the pretty girl, even if she dresses in jeans one size too big and wears boyfriend sweaters. Fuck one, fuck all, no way out of that. So maybe I fucked more than one, but it feels so good. Like amazing good. Like, "if I could do this every day I would" kinda good. But there's a pretty girl game in high school and I'm learning how to play it. Soon, I'll have it mastered, then get out of this place so I never have to play this game again. Nope, once I'm out, I'm out. Valleyfield can kiss my ass. And all the girls, and parents, and teachers, can kiss my ass too. But I'm still here...the game goes on.

It's coming close to the end. Amanda's the only real friend I care about. We've both had our moments, Amanda and I. But I've been a good friend to her. I helped her get through her whole mom running out thing. She didn't even want to come back to school after that, but I called her everyday, texted her from class every minute, invited her out to the field parties and didn't make her pay for any drugs.

When she wanted to get out but didn't want to be seen, I took her for hooch cruises on the highway. We rolled up joints or smoked from a pipe her mom left back from a trip to Toronto years before.

Sunday I'd bring her with me to help out with the group I started for kids with 'mental health problems.' Alcoholic parents meant they had FAS. Abused girls getting into fights at recess meant they were violent. Not getting any attention at home and talking too much in class meant ADHD. I don't actually think they had mental health issues, just really messed up lives. I just saw a bunch of kids with no one to really talk to, no one that understood how to speak their language or got their humour. They were screaming.

Whispers, whispers, whispers. Small town whispers turn anthills into Everest. If your crazy parents didn't make you crazy, everyone whispering about your crazy parents sure would.

"Why do they call you 'Treasure?'" there's always one brave boy.

"Because that's my name."

"Your real name?"

"That's what my mom tells me."

"That name is perfect."

"And you're a darling."

Being a 16-year-old talking to boys who were like 12 and 13 was kind of odd because I still knew what it felt like to be them; I didn't even really have to remember. Like I knew exactly what they were thinking before they were even thinking it. They were easy.

I had to be more clever with the girls, though. I knew one look at me and they'd think I thought my shit smelled like flowers. So, I never dressed up; no makeup, only tights or jeans a couple sizes too big and sweaters and t-shirts even bigger. They needed someone who they could admire but was in no way intimidating.

Halfway through the year I won a grant to fund my program. We moved up out of the church into this hall that seniors used twice a week to play bingo. Amanda was feeling much better by then, and she made sure she was with me every time we met with our group.

"BAGS," Amanda said.

"BAGS?"

"Yeah, let's call the group BAGS. It says here on the form you need an organization name, so let's call it BAGS."

"And... does that mean something?"

"Boys And Girls Screaming."

***

There he is again. This time he's waiting for me outside the hospital, standing next to a garbage bin with one leg up against the wall.

"Why are you in there?" he asks. "Are you hurt?"

"I was hurt, but now I'm fine. Now I'm beautiful."

"What do you mean?"

"I mean everyone looks at me now. Everyone gives me attention. They see me."

We keep talking, longer this time. I tell him I'll be leaving the hospital soon. He asks if we'll see each other again.

"We're dreaming," I say. "This is just a dream. You are just a dream. None of this is happening."

My eyes open. Back to my life. Confused by these dreams but thinking about my father.

Both are just as puzzling. I wonder who this boy can be. I wonder how it can be the same boy over and over again. I wonder if it's all real.

And my father. It's hard to read him now. He spends a lot of time just sitting and staring, scrolling through his cell phone and just staring. We never speak about it, the accident. He comes into my room sometimes when I get home from school and I can tell he wants to say something. I can tell because my dad doesn't hesitate. He has the opposite problem, always doing or saying something without thinking about it first. So, when he rolls into my room thinking about what to say, I know. We both know.

Tragedy staring right at me. The cost of my beauty fumbling his words. I think, would I ever give it back? Would I ever give back being beautiful for my father to stand up and walk out of that wheelchair? All this power...gone, just so my father could be his regular coke sniffing, late night, non-drug addict/drug addict self again?

My dad hasn't walked the same since. He eventually got a cane, but still uses the wheelchair more than he should. He skips rehab three times a week and barely moves around at all inside the house. It's hard to say, and even more difficult to accept, but he was better as a drug addict. I know Mom feels the same way but she'd never come out and say it. None of us would.

Would I take it back?

Would I give up these dreams? They must mean something, right? All dreams have meaning. It can't be a coincidence that these dreams started after my accident. And why would I be dreaming about the same person? A boy I've never met in real life but who's important enough to infiltrate my subconscious thoughts.

We talk in our dreams. We talk to each other. I remember these quiet conversations when I wake up. I ask my mom and she says it's called a recurring dream. A dream you have again and again. I tell her it's not the same dream, though, only the same person.

"It's the same thing, Treasure. Just a recurring dream." So, I drop it. I don't mention my dreams to either of my parents again. They have enough going on right now. Ever since my accident, there's been this visible distance between them. I just watch them, sometimes. I watch my mom and dad exist in this odd manner. They speak mostly in question and answer format, my mom usually the initiator.

"Did you remember to stop by Alvin and check those brakes, Tommy?"

"Yes, I did."

"I'll be staying late at school today. Can you get home on time so Treasure's not here by herself?"

"Yes, I can."

"Where'd I put my goddam cane?"

"Left it right beside the kitchen table, Tommy."

That's it. Mostly, anyways. Sometimes at night, before the accident, Mom would sit on Dad's lap and they'd watch TV in between pecks. But I never caught them making out in the kitchen, or sneaking off to the bedroom way too early to be going to sleep.

They were just parents. Friends who grew up together, who knew each other's parents since before they had pubic hair. To say they were miserable would be a lie. But I wouldn't jump to say they were happy either.

And now this. Now dad is home all the time rolling around in his wheelchair or limping with his cane. He makes heaving sounds every time he gets out of his wheelchair to lay on the couch. He eats dinner in front of the TV now. Mom just watches him.

It doesn't make sense. The mood of the house doesn't make sense. I'm alive, breathing, looking and feeling better than ever. My dad is alive, breathing, not quite himself, but he did save my life and didn't die doing it.

Where's the celebration?

Nothing even close. Evenings are peaceful now; quiet. My parents are polite to one another. It seems both of them are somehow scarred by my accident, yet I can't figure out why. And my dad is just gliding further and further away while my mom sinks deeper and deeper into herself.

All of this happening in silence. No outbursts, no eruptions, no domestic disturbances. No explanation.

JUSTIN

Everyone keeps asking me if I'm OK. I guess losing both parents at the same time should've had a more visible impact on me. I should've been depressed. I should've be moping around in that basement forever. I shouldn't have had to worry about working because the insurance money means I'm good for the next twenty years of my life.

"It's OK not to be OK, Justin." My aunt.

"Take your time, Justin. Don't rush into anything right now." An older cousin.

"You stay as long as you like, Justin. We are family and we'll get through this together." My grandmother. I only last there for a week before I want to rip my hair out. Sitting in that house everyday, watching her cook the same food as her daughter, listening to her subtle frustration with her husband, it's all too much.

So, I leave. Take only the jeans and shirt I'm wearing and get up out of there. I tell my grandparents I need a few days to myself, but I've already put first and last down on an apartment on Queen Street. The building is only a couple years old, and the managers are both really cool. It's only the second place I've looked at but I know right away.

Not that I had all these high expectations. I just needed the building to be clean and wanted to be close to some action. Check and check, so I give them two cheques. I knew how upset my grandparents will be if I told them the truth. They'll try their best to talk me out of it. Tell me I'm making a mistake. Be worried that I'll spend all my money and end up on the street or something.

All those things could be true. I really have no idea what I'm doing. How could I? I'm still a teenager and have never been on my own before. I didn't even know where to start when I decided I wanted out of my grandparents' place. It was Steve who came to my rescue. Told me I'd need a job letter or some proof of income. We thought about making a fake, but when I showed the building manager my bank account statement, it was "Sign on the dotted line."

Steve was also the excuse for my grandparents. I told them I'd be staying with him for a few days and they were cool about it. In those few days, we basically furnished my entire place. Most of the stuff we ordered online. I found a cool coffee table at a condo sale and a lamp I put in my living room on Bunz. The entire process was a lot less painful than I'd thought it would be.

Of course, I'm sure having Steve with me has something to do with that. He never once asks me about how I'm feeling. He isn't extra nice to me and I never feel he's doing anything out of pity. He's just being Steve, my friend, my brother. That's all I want. Soon, we'll be doing the same thing for him when he gets tired of jumping from parent to parent and moves out too.

It's crazy how your life can mimic those around you even when your circumstances are completely different. Even when your personalities are completely different. But being different is what makes us work. Steve gets to be Steve, and I get to be me.

Needless to say, my grandparents are pretty ticked off once I tell them the truth.

"You're making a mistake, Justin. You need to be with your family right now. You're still a kid."

I think they're more disappointed than anything. My grandmother doesn't take the news well at all. She isn't just upset that I basically just ran away or that I was telling them over the phone rather than in person. What I know put her over the top is the fact that she feels like she can't help me. I'm her daughter's only child. Her only grandchild by blood. And she can't help me.

She's right, though. No one can help me and I don't want anyone trying. I'm not sure what makes me feel that way. I'm not sure why I want to be alone when I have a family that cares so much. But it's how I feel. It's what I need. Even if I don't know what I'm doing, I want to make my own decisions.

Speaking of decisions, I make another one. I decide I wouldn't waste all this insurance money. My parents worked way too hard to give me a good life for me to go spend all of it on bullshit. I've given myself three months. In that time, I have to find a real job that can pay my rent and all my bills. I also decide that in those three months, I won't spend any of this money on drugs. As tempting as it is, I can't wrap my mind around using this gift from my parents to get high.

And I don't. Instead I write down a few things I think I'd like to do.

- ~~Manager for a clothing store~~
- ~~Model~~
- Graphic designer
- ~~Open a bar~~
- Travel
- ~~Food critic~~
- ~~Photographer~~

I scratch out the ones that are just stupid. I also put a line through any that won't make me any money right away. Travel is still a real option. The thought of really getting away makes so much sense. But that would be breaking my promise of not spending any more of the insurance money, so I reluctantly push that idea to the side. Don't have the heart to scratch it out, though. I'll get to it one day.

That leaves me with graphic design. It's something I did through most of high school, anyways. I just do it for fun, though, and never really took any classes on it. I figure if I want to get paid for it, I have to at least get some kind of formal training.

School isn't going to happen, so my formal training consists of daily YouTube videos and two weekend courses. That's pretty much it. I start applying to a bunch of different agencies and hope for a call back. Two phone interviews and one in-person interview later and still no job. I'm not discouraged or anything. I'm enjoying all of this, like life has been put back into my own.

It takes my grandmother to make it happen, though. Pretty randomly, I go over on a Saturday for dinner and tell her about my job hunting.

"I just wanna do something I'm good at, Grandma. I don't wanna get stuck doing something just for money or something that's gonna put my mind on autopilot."

She looks at me like I'm a typical, naive Millennial, but that doesn't stop her from supporting me.

"My friend Donna has a daughter who just started her own advertising agency. I'll give her a call on Monday."

That's all it takes. A week after my grandmother put in that call, I'm working my first real full time job, and I'm still here. A promise kept. I haven't touched a penny of that money since.

***

I get my first tattoo in Kensington, the first names of my mom and my dad on each middle knuckle. It's painful, and I have to stop more than once because it hurts that much. But I figure my hands are the one part of my body I'll see the most of each day. Especially now that I'm doing graphic design, I won't go a day without seeing my parents.

I still haven't cried. Not in real life, anyways. Only in my dreams. Only with her.

"They're gone," I say.

"Who's gone?"

"My parents. They're dead. Both of them."

She doesn't say anything. We stand beside each other in emptiness, leaned up against what feels like a tree. It's the first time we hold hands. It's the first time I cry. She still has no words but her being there makes me feel safe. Safe enough to shed tears. Safe enough to let her in.

In real life, it takes half a dozen people to make me feel safe. It takes people filing in and out of my apartment from Thursday to Sunday for me to not feel alone. Then sometimes all I want is to be alone. All I want is my phone to stop vibrating, people to stop knocking on my door, the music turned off.

Where's the peace, I think. Through the chaos or the solitude, nothing really makes me feel anything. I don't know what to make of myself right now. Something's telling me I should be grieving more, or grieving differently. I'm not even sure if I'm grieving at all anymore.

Whatever. Who has time to be psychoanalyzing themselves? Not me, not right now. Right now, it's about life. Right now, it's about texting Steve and figuring out what's on for this weekend. Doesn't matter what kind of mood I'm in, Steve makes it better.

Another tattoo. This time more ostentatious. Louder. "ALL OR NOTHING." Don't ask me why because I really don't know the answer. It seems like the right thing to do. And a statement like that needs the right platform. What better platform than my back, the entire thing, almost. This one doesn't hurt as much, though. I get it done in one shot.

It feels good, too. When I sit up from the table, I feel this huge sense of accomplishment. Like if I've won something. Steve says it's stupid. I don't completely disagree, but stupidity has its place, too.

***

Thinking back to my life before my parents died, I wonder if I'd even recognize myself now. I really wonder if on my first day of school in grade nine, walking through the hallways feeling like everyone was staring at me walking alone, judging me for being a bit too tall, a bit too skinny, for my hair not being perfectly combed, or my uniform just not fitting right. All of these thoughts happening with every single step.

I begged my parents not to send me to private school, even cried the night before to my mom hoping she'd feel some kind of sudden sympathy and tell my father how terrible of an idea this was. I wanted to go to Central Tech, or Humberside, or even Western Tech, anywhere but private school.

"This is what's best, Justin," was all my mom said, barely even looking up from her laptop. "You should be happy you're going to one of the best schools in the city."

"But none of my friends will be there."

"That's not a bad thing, Justin. And you can still see your friends after school or on the weekend. We're not stopping you from hanging out with them." She closes her laptop and stands up to face me. "Listen, I know it seems like a big deal now, like not being around your friends all day is the worst thing in the world. But you'll be fine. You'll make new friends and a few weeks from now you'll forget about this entire conversation."

I wasn't convinced. The next morning my mom had to drag me out of bed. She literally pulled off my blanket and held a cup of water tilted over my head.

"It's either you shower in the bathroom or shower right here."

Standing in the shower, I tried to wrap my mind around what was about to happen, what I was about to step into. "This is a good thing," I repeated to myself. "I'll be fine, stop worrying." Fifteen minutes later and my mom was pounding on the door. "You need to be dressed and ready to go in five minutes."

No, actually, I wasn't going to be OK. I hated this, hated the fact I'd be going to some private school I never heard of. Hated my mom for blowing me off the night before and the months before that of pleading almost daily for her to change her mind. For both of them to change their minds.

It was hard because in a way I was actually happy. Happy that my dad's business finally took off. That we went from living in a basement when I was in first and second grade, to renting a semi-detached up till 6th grade, then finally buying a four bedroom home the summer before grade 8.

That was the dream, right? That is what families dream of. To come from nothing to something; from the basement to the biggest house on the block. My parents were in their mid-forties when this all happened, my dad closer to fifty. At first it didn't feel like much changed. I was still an only child, I always had my own room, the house we bought was in the same neighbourhood, and last I checked, our last name was still Soares.

My mom did throw a few more parties. Well, adult versions of parties with soft music with no lyrics, wine and some food no real person could possibly eat. I did notice a few people I'd never seen before, or never even heard my parents speak of. But that was about it for change.

Till this, of course. Till me sitting in the middle rows of class off to the side of the room, either staring at the blackboard or pretending to be listening to every word the teacher was saying.

I wonder. I really, really, wonder if I would recognize myself.

Is it possible to go an entire school day without talking? The correct answer is "Yes!" It's very possible and exactly how I spent my first day of ninth grade. That did nothing for my enthusiasm and I didn't speak to my parents that night, either.

Day 2. Sitting in the middle row off to the side again. Class hadn't started yet but Mrs. Blake was writing something on the board.

"Hey." A voice from somewhere behind me. No one knew me, I didn't know anyone, so I didn't turn around.

"Hey. Justin, right?" I turned my head.

"See that girl over there?" I followed his head motion to the front of the class on the opposite side of the room.

"Don't look now," he said abruptly. "She thinks you're cute. Said I should invite you to her house party this weekend."

"House party? I don't even know who she is." He looked at me like I fell from another planet.

"You're funny, Justin. Well...look at her now, look at her real good. Then let me know after class if you really wanna turn her down."

I spoke a lot more that day. I found out my messenger's name was Steve, that my admirer's name was Cait, and that I was about to go to my first high school house party.

Convincing my mom to let me go didn't take any convincing at all. She was glad I made friends so quickly. I was glad when Steve said we could go together. When we got there, I found out it wasn't actually Cait's party. It was her 16-year-old sister's, Amber. Me, Cait, and Steve were the only 9th graders there, there being a house on a side street off Avenue road. A house that resembled mine only in size, but looked more like a classic mansion, with large wooden French doors protected by two rows of some kind of tree I didn't know the name of. It was more like walking into a country club instead of a house in midtown Toronto.

Cait opened the door and my instinct was to run away. My palms instantly got moist. My heart was ready to spring out of my chest and my eyes wouldn't blink. Not even for a quarter of a second did I want to miss any part of that scene, of Cait standing in the doorway in a black tank top and leaf green skirt that stopped short enough to drive any teenager to insanity.

Steve caught me apparently lost in another world and nudged me with his elbow. Cait grabbed my hand and without taking her eyes away from mine, guided me inside.

"I like your shirt." I paused not knowing if she was being sarcastic or giving me a real compliment.

"Thanks," I said, figuring that was the appropriate answer either way. Then Cait whispered in my ear without breaking stride, "How hard you gonna make me work to get it off?"

She didn't wait for me to answer, she just smiled and kept walking us through the party.

A few brief introductions later and I was already drunk. Cait kept handing me drinks and I kept downing them, one after the other not really thinking about anything else except the fact that I had Cait's full attention all night. I saw other guys sneaking peeks at us, wondering who the hell I was and how the hell I was managing to keep the prize of the party all to myself.

"You ready?" Cait's question was more like a challenge, like a coach would ask his players in the locker room before the championship game. Again, she didn't wait for me to answer, just led me away from the fray, off to a side room that she opened with a key tucked in her skirt pocket.

As soon as the room door opened, she pushed herself on me, pressing her lips directly on my own, easily unbuttoning the shirt she questioned earlier in the evening. I tried mimicking the pattern of her lips, stuck my tongue out when I felt hers, unbuttoned my pants and lifted her skirt.

I'd never done any of this before but it all felt natural. For whatever reason, maybe the alcohol, maybe the marijuana, I was the most calm I'd been all night. It wasn't the last time I'd be in Cait's house, in that specific room, making out and more. But that first time was the first time I knew.

***

I saw her again. In the hospital this time. I was worried. I could feel in my dream that I was worried. But that's not possible, is it? To feel emotions in dreams. And I'm realizing this isn't the first time I've seen her, or dreamed of seeing her.

The first time was on the lake sitting on rocks, or maybe in the sand. It was the end of my waterfall dream. We stared at each other. Her eyes were the same colour as the water. We spoke. I asked her if I'd see her again. But it always ended before any answer.

At the hospital I asked if she was OK. She said she was getting better. It's not making any sense, but by then we've seen each other so many times, been in each other's dreams so many times. It can only be real, right? She has to be real, doesn't she?

Steve became my brother. He's an only child, too, so we for real become brothers. He grew up split between the Annex and Forest Hill, sharing time with divorced parents whose days revolved around work and arguing about who kept Steve on weekends. Didn't make any sense since Steve spent most of his time with the nanny, regardless of whose house he was at.

Soon he was at my place more than anywhere else. He had his own seat at our dinner table and clothes in one of our guest rooms. He called my parents Mom and Pop. Family by everything but birth.

High school without Steve would've been treacherous, or at least that's what I tell myself. He made it bearable almost from day one. He was my partner. Or I should say I was his. He introduced me to everyone I knew, took me to my first party, helped me seal the deal on my first girlfriend.

Not sure I can call Cait much of a girlfriend, though. I mean she was my first, and we'd mess around all throughout high school, but there was never any expectation of commitment. We had fun together. All four of us did. I experienced my first acid trip at Cait and Amber's place. Another weekend their parents were away. It was Steve's idea.

"You never forget your first trip," he said.

"So, you've done this before," I asked.

He laughed. "I did it last week."

High school. It's like an experiment gone bad. I picture scientists and researchers in white robes standing somewhere behind glass windows, observing, taking notes. Some of them think it's a bad idea and want to stop the experiment.

"Nothing good can come from lumping male and female adolescents together." Head *nods and head shakes.*

"Their hormones are out of control." More nods and shakes.

Some want to test variables.

"Let's see what happens if we make them think drugs are cool." Oohs and ahhs.

"I say we ban any condoms or contraception from the school grounds." Full applause.

Craziness. I just left high school and am already forgetting what it was like. I remember some moments, of course, Steve being the common denominator in most of them. He made me, me. Helped me see what others saw.

"People like you," He'd say. "You barely say a word and people still like you." This must have been odd for Steve. He was the type to know homeless people on Queen Street by name. He could walk into a room and spark a conversation with anyone, male or female, and make it like they grew up on the same block.

"Yeah but you can walk into a room and get that same attention without saying anything. You're tall, you have long hair, and you're awkward. Win, win, win. If you played an instrument girls would throw their panties at you."

Maybe, I thought. But by the end of high school those maybes were gone. I kept my mysterious demeanor, but added Steve's confidence. Approaching girls became easy as rolling a joint, and the high nearly the same.

Steve never changed. To this day, he never changed. I wonder what he thinks sometimes, how he feels knowing who I used to be. Knowing I went from librarian to Lord Byron. From the boy he dragged to his first party, to us both doing straights for lunch in the bathroom stalls.

I never felt like I changed that much, just got comfortable. When I got cool with the people around me it felt OK to be myself. But that sounds like bullshit. Right now, I could feel at home in a bar full of strangers. I know this, I've tried it many times before. I think it was symbolic I lost my virginity during my first week of grade nine to one of the hottest girls in the school. It became a sort of myth around my peers that turned me into this semi-legendary figure.

Then all I had to do was play the role. Mostly I pretended at first. Stayed quiet and let the hallways tell its own tales. But I guess I figured I had to start living up to all the rumors, so I did. It's easy to play a part when it's already been written. When you don't have to make anything up, just read from the script. I read the script, then became the writer. And Steve was the producer through it all. Disney himself.

Sometimes I think I take things too far, though. And I know he feels the same way. He tells me sometimes, with a sideways kind of approach.

"You don't always have to be 'on', Justin. The world would understand if you took a day or two from being you." Or "Why don't you just sit this one out, Justin? You have a lifetime of Friday nights."

But you don't get 'ALL OR NOTHING' tattooed on your back if you have an off switch. And I certainly don't. My green light runs on Duracell. There's just something in me. Something. I can't place it. And it's not like I'm loud. I don't dance. I don't jump on chairs in clubs. I don't even go to clubs. I just like being present, in the mix. I like the energy of crowds, streetcar bells and GO train horns.

And I like being around females. Understatement. I love being around females. Beautiful ones, any chance I get and as much as possible. And they like being around me. I'm not that guy scared to start a conversation, but I don't always feel like I have to make an impression.

I just play it cool. Not intentionally. I don't play some part hoping to get laid down the road. And even though that's what ends up happening most of the time, it's not often that sex is the sustaining part to the connection. And if it is, it's because the sex is really fucking amazing.

But so is company. So is sitting on my balcony facing the CN tower drinking wine at 1 in the morning. Or adult colouring at the Gladstone on a Thursday evening listening to live music.

Steve thinks I'm crazy. Not like looney crazy, just, like, too in love with life crazy. One time I tried to tell him about these dreams I've been having. These dreams about this girl, the same girl over and over again since my parents died.

I tell him we speak in our dreams. We've seen each other grow the last few years. I tell him I can describe her, and that we talk about meeting in real life one day. He says I'm nuts.

"That's just your Romeo side talking. You would love nothing more than for there to be one person in this world made just for you. And of course, she's the most beautiful girl you've ever seen, right?"

I tell him yes, but then he reminds me of Cait. How I thought for a year straight I'd never meet anyone as beautiful, till I met Mackenzie. Then Mackenzie changed my life till she introduced me to her cousin. I don't remember her cousin's name, but she let me do whatever I wanted with her and never said a word to Mackenzie.

But *"So what?"* I tell myself. These dreams are real. She is real. Real as all the other beautiful women I've known and been with. And I don't care what Steve says. One day we will meet, and that will be it for me. I know it.

TREASURE

The smell of the rain is what keeps my window open. The smell that took me back to Daddy's sail boat on those gusty August mornings. The sun would barely have peaked over Lake Huron when we'd push off from shore. A cup of hot chocolate is all we'd need to set us off for hours, most of it silent, the wind more of a companion than our own voices. And the smell, the smell of the lake I could only describe as a feeling; the feeling of a ten-year-old girl far away from everything.

It's been years since we've been on that sailboat. Even before my accident, we'd cut back on our trips. I never told my dad how much I loved those mornings. How deeply they're etched in my memory. He probably thinks I don't care. Or maybe he didn't need whatever he was getting from those morning sails across the lake anymore.

Now those mornings aren't even possible. Standing too long has become difficult for my dad. Walking is a chore and any other action requiring his legs is almost impossible. Impossible because that's how he's made it because he's never cared to get better.

A full year after my accident and he still hasn't made much progress. We haven't made much progress. And I still haven't asked the question that's been stuck in my mind from the first time I opened my eyes on that hospital bed.

Too much time had passed now for me to worry about whether or not my dad was ready to speak about what I saw that night; the woman he dragged out the bar. The real cause, or so I reasoned.

The day before I leave for the University of Toronto, on a full academic scholarship no less, on one of those gusty August mornings when he's already perched outside on his wheelchair, I pull up a chair beside him.

My thoughts are on leaving Valleyfield, on my future life waiting for me in Toronto. A life that's been calling since we took our first trip to the city to visit my mother's cousin when I was only in grade five. Most of my friends talked about the buildings, about how tall they were and how many of them lined the city. But what stuck out to me were the people, the variations of people. Dark and light brown, pale and tanned, caramel, freckled face, some black like the tires of our SUV, others mixed in indescribable combinations.

You don't see that in Valleyfield. Mainly you come across Boulay's and Boudreau's, Bennett's and Imhoff's, many of whom speaking dialects of French most Parisians wouldn't recognize. But no melting pot here, no mosaic of cultures I heard Toronto was famous for; not in Valleyfield. The only discernable difference are the Christians, devout rigid Evangelical Christians with sons and daughters who are expected to fill the church every Sunday and wait till marriage to consummate any relationship. Christians who gawk at divorce despite regular infidelities. Whose advice to their children is always, "Pray to God," or "Let Jesus be your guide" to solve their problems because only He knows the way.

These are the same daughters who come to Valleyfield High and say anal or oral is OK because only vaginal penetration counts as sex. The same sons who know porn stars by name and get married at twenty so they could feel better about the last three years they spent having sex in back seats.

I'm so ready to let it all go. To leave all of it behind me and run far, far away. Can you imagine the frustration of feeling disconnected from the very place you are growing up? I mean consciously disconnected. Like waking up everyday and knowing this isn't where you're meant to be. Knowing these people will never understand you because they aren't supposed to. Years and years of waiting to disappear from this place.

Now that time is finally here. My last year of high school was my best. I was so close and didn't want anything preventing me from leaving. I got A's, and not just A's but A pluses. I stopped texting in class, stopped eyeing boys in the hallway, finished all my homework on time; stuff I wouldn't think possible even a year before.

My grades were always good before that, like I got some A's and mostly B's with only one or two grades lower than that. I never failed any classes, was never suspended or outwardly rude to teachers. I just never really tried. Finding the right colour for my hair was more important than any assignment. Figuring out how to sneak in and out of boys' houses before their parents got home was more exciting than any fieldtrip. I was a teenager.

The only thing I genuinely had a hard time with before leaving Valleyfield was saying goodbye to the BAGS. We'd become family, literally, because they'd all hated their own. On our last day together they baked cupcakes, each of them choosing their favourite colour icing to sign their name. They walked up to me one by one with paper bags over each of their little faces, decorated to their tastes with jaggedly cut holes showing their eyes.

Amanda had organized it on her own, getting the BAGS together the week before. I fought back the tears, tried to anyway. But when they all circled around to hug me and say their goodbyes, tears were all I could manage.

"I'll keep it going," Amanda promised. "We can't all be honour students. And they need this. The town needs this."

We just wrapped our arms around each other and kept crying. I hadn't realized how close Amanda and I had gotten. How much time we spent together and how much I would miss her.

"You should come with me," I told her the next day. "Toronto has tons of colleges and stuff, just come with me. We don't have to go to the same school to stay friends."

"Maybe next semester," Amanda said. "Go test it out and see what you think. Then we'll see what happens."

It's only today I found out from my dad, who was friendly with Amanda's dad, that she also applied and got accepted into UofT.

"She chose to stay here," my dad told me sitting there in his wheelchair on the porch. "That might be hard for you to understand, but it was her decision."

It wasn't hard at all, actually. As much as all my friends complained about Valleyfield and their urge to leave, most, no actually nearly all of them will end up staying. That's just the reality of it. It all sounds good when we're in our rooms or in our basements dreaming about what living in Toronto must be like. But leaving, like actually leaving and having to start over, meet new people, make new friends, find restaurants you like, probably room with someone you don't like, be away from your family, your dog—only a few really make it out because only a few genuinely want to make it out.

Amanda was as much a part of Valleyfield as the four walls we dreamed in growing up, with the same chance of leaving. I was already on my way out, but needed to know the truth from my father.

He was uneasy in his wheelchair, shifting like he was trying to fix his car seat after someone else had driven it.

"Who was she dad? And why'd you throw her round like that?"

***

Treasure Coliette Zahariah, daughter of Thomas Zahariah and supposed daughter of Kay Marie Boulay Zahariah. I want to put that in writing, on my birth certificate, on my driver's license, on the attendance sheet at school. Everywhere my name is written down, I need it to be known that my mother is not my mother. I want it to be known that I don't in fact know who my mother is. That I've been lied to for 18 years. Eighteen fucking years.

Who does that? Who lies to their kid for that long? Even when I would ask what I thought were stupid questions like "Why do I have freckles, Mommy?" or "Daddy, how come you and Mommy don't get this dark in the summer?" Stupid, dumb, naive, kid questions. And then get stupid, dumb, manipulative, adult answers like, "Your great grandfather had some freckles," or "Skin complexion skips generations, Treasure." Really? Skips generations? Right.

I feel...I feel like I don't really know how to feel, or what to think, or who or what to believe. I asked my mother, the only mother I knew, or thought I knew, if what my dad said was true. If she really isn't my mother. If that entire story of my birth in the back of dad's car which he still owned was all a lie.

Of course, I didn't believe all of it, not even most of it. But to know it was all a fucking lie? Like the entire story was nothing but lie on top of lie, complete make belief...

"Is it true?"

The woman whom I had called mother for 18 years, who had probably envisioned this moment, hid from it, mimicked it in her mind over and over again, now just stands under the arch of her bedroom door, staring at nothing in particular, much like my dad did when he wheeled himself out to the front porch. She looks prepared, even though I can tell she's uneasy. Even though her and my dad had discussed telling me before I went away, that they decided it had to be done before I left for Toronto. That I had to know the truth.

"The truth is that I am your mother," she finally responds.

"Don't do that. Don't you even think about doing that. Are you really my mother? Did you give birth to me?"

"I did not give birth to you, but yes I am your mother. The only mother you've known."

"And why is that? Why are you the only mother I've ever known? Why is the only time I've ever seen my real mother is when my father dragged her out of a bar?"

I cover my face, cupping it with both hands and fall to my knees. "I hate this, I fucking hate this!"

I don't know what is making me this emotional, why I'm sobbing on the floor with the mother I love stroking my hair, wrapping her arms around me, helping me to my room, her own tears falling faint. I say this because part of me doesn't care who my real mother is. Even in these moments curled over on the floor, something in me wonders why I'm doing this, why this makes me so upset.

I know being lied to for 18 years is definitely part of it. I know having them tell me the day before I leave to go hundreds of miles away to start a new chapter of my life is also part of it. I think just knowing...no I think just knowing sooner would've helped me deal with this on my feet. The suddenness of it all, the fact that I won't have time to probe my parents, to ask a new question every time one pops into my head, to have them play nice for the next six months while I suck up all the extra attention, to have the chance to pretend I'm still deeply hurt, long after I resign within myself that I really don't give a shit.

And I really don't. Even laying in my room for hours after confronting my mom, I know I'm not prepared to take things much further. I won't set out on a moral journey to find my birth mother, pretending I need to know who she is so I can fill some part of me I felt was missing all my life. None of that is true.

The truth is I'm happy. I've been mostly happy for all of my life. And the one thing that brings me the most discomfort, stirs the most anxiety or causes me any unhappiness is about to be a distant memory, literally. The thought of leaving for Toronto is actually what calms me down, what makes me get up from my bed, grab my makeup bag, and head for the bathroom.

I let too much foundation and smoky eyes stop my tears; a new pink lip gloss I didn't plan on cracking till I got to my dorm boosts my spirits; and a perfume that smelled like sweet honey that my mother—this mother—bought me the first day I came home after my accident, I let that make me smile. I barely used it before now, and sometimes I just pumped it into the air to remind me of who I'd become since walking out of that hospital.

"Don't you like it, Treasure? I can get you a different scent." She asked me this after I'd been home for a few months and the bottle was still full.

"I love it actually. I just don't wanna use it too much. I like looking at it on my dresser."

"You know they made more than one, right? I can always just get you another one."

"I'm not sure you can."

***

My parents weren't the only ones dishing out secrets before I left Valleyfield. I needed someone else to know about my dreams. Someone who wouldn't dismiss me as delusional or make me feel like I'm losing my mind. Even with my intentions of telling Amanda, it still took some convincing.

"You're not gonna believe me." I don't even know how this conversation got started.

"You're just gonna think I'm crazy." Amanda kept begging me to tell her about my dreams. She's just told me everything about her weird dream about being covered in snowflakes.

"Not snow," she says. "Snowflakes."

Now I guess it's my turn. Thinking about it is weird enough. Having to tell someone else about a boy I saw in my dreams almost every night for the past couple years is just totally uncomfortable.

"I don't know what to say. It's just a dream, right? He's a boy I only see in my dreams. But we talk to each other. Like back and forth conversations. And we talk about stuff that's happening in our real lives. Like I remember telling him about being in the hospital after my accident."

"And he would say things back? Like, did he remember you were in the hospital the next time you saw him?"

"Yeah, that's the craziest part. We both remember everything from all our dreams together. At first it was kind of blurry. Like we couldn't remember everything clearly. But then we just clicked. Every dream we just pick right back up where we left off the last time."

Amanda is all into this.

"So, what's his name?"

"OK, so that's the thing. Some things are still dreamlike. So, when we're in our dream, we don't know our own names or where we're from. We can describe stuff that's been happening, but our dream world is what we know most. It's where we exist and build memories. It's just...strange."

Strange is probably the best way to describe how I feel revealing this stuff to Amanda. But not because she's judging or anything, it's because explaining my dreams out loud makes me realize how insane all of this really is.

And, to be honest, it made me feel a bit stupid because in telling Amanda about these dreams, I realize something else.

"You like this guy." Amanda says it first.

"I like a lot of guys." I'm not about to give in that easy. "You can't like someone that isn't real. I mean you can, but I like him in the same way you like a character in a movie. It's fun while you're watching it, but once the movie's over, it's back to real life."

VOL. II

TREASURE

Toronto. Finally. The city looks even more incredible now that I'm staying. The buildings look that much taller, the lights that much brighter, the cars, cranes, horns, airplanes; all sounds, beautiful sounds, almost unfamiliar but all of them adding to my excitement at finally arriving to where would be my home forever.

And I do mean that. Forever. Both my parents knew I was never coming back, that's why they told me what they did before I left. They knew they would have to take the hours long trip from Valleyfield to Toronto if they ever hoped to see me again. They knew that the moment I got accepted into UofT. I knew that long before then.

Is it wrong that I'm this comfortable with not seeing my parents for years at a time? That I want to be out of Valleyfield so bad I would sacrifice damn near anything? Anyone? Friendships, relationships, any kind of emotional connection gone just so I could get to the city I knew would appreciate what it meant to be me.

And it sounds a little dramatic, maybe even a bit naive. Putting all this pressure on a city I barely know, a city I know only through my expectations, my assumptions, through Google searches and a few brief visits during my childhood. But that's what makes Toronto exciting—not knowing exactly what I was getting myself into. Driving down the highway and seeing the Yorkdale sign, wondering about what stores are inside and how people are dressed. Wondering how I would dress myself now that I was away from the judgement of the eyes on every corner.

That has to be the most exciting of all the exciting parts of being in Toronto. Not knowing anyone. Knowing that none of these eyes were familiar. Knowing I could be whoever I wanted to be, be with whoever I wanted to be with, without the weight of the consequences of my actions be validated to each set of eyes in Valleyfield.

I wondered what this me would look like. How I would wear my hair, who I would hang out with; which of these boys would I be most attracted to?

"Finally," I say. "Finally, finally, finally."

One thing quickly dawned on me, though. I'm not the only beautiful girl in the city. Toronto is filled with girls who are just splendid. Girls who wear black tuques with coloured hair tucked underneath with plain white vests and tattoos. Girls who ride bicycles in dresses with a helmet. These girls aren't even trying and still take my breath away.

But it all seems so normal for everyone else. No guys freak out, barely even turning their heads when they pass these flawless females. Of course, they get hit on, but if I was a guy, I'd be losing my mind. I wouldn't even know where to start.

How is this possible? All these treasures in one city. How does an average girl get laid out here? Well, dumb question, guys stick their things in anything. But still, must be rough to be ugly in Toronto. To not have anything going for you. You'd have to do a lot just for some scraps.

Truth is, this actually makes me feel good. No more big-fish-small-pond problems. I can swim freely in the ocean, just part of a school of other swimmers avoiding bait. Or taking a bite whenever I feel like it.

Plus, I still have my moments. Times when I'm sitting on the streetcar daydreaming, staring out the window, then come to because I feel someone looking at me. Or my dorm mates asking me what it feels like to be me, to know I could get a guy to do anything I wanted.

It's always different when a girl lets you know how good you look. We're wired in the opposite direction; to criticize every lash, every heel, every hair colour, anything that makes us feel better about looking the way we do. So, to hear another female dig deep inside her hater soul and dish out a compliment, you know there's something there. Something a bit magical, mystical. Some kind of treasure.

I have one of those experiences on the streetcar. This girl is just flat out staring at me.

Well wait, girl is the wrong word. This is a woman. I can tell by her heels and her purse that she's one of those women who looks a lot younger than she probably is. Either way, the streetcar is full enough that we both have to stand, but empty enough that we can see each other clearly. She stands facing me. I stand holding the pole pretending not to notice. But then she walks right up to me.

"I'm sorry," she says. "I know I shouldn't stare, but I'm sure you know how beautiful you are."

I feel nervous. Odd because I'm used to compliments, but this seems so bold. Plus, we're on the streetcar with a bunch of other rubberneckers trying their best to pretend they aren't hearing every word.

"Thank you," is all I can muster. She doesn't move, just smiles back and reaches her fingers to the tips of my hair. I felt my neck heat up. I want to pull away but just stand there. More gazes now. The pretending from the spectators is over.

"Umm, stop me if this is too forward, but I'd like to see you again. Outside of this streetcar, I mean." This time she whispers, quiet enough that it feels like our secret. I don't know what to say. I don't have to say anything. She hands me her business card from out of her purse and gets off at the next stop.

I go to my apartment that night and enjoy myself, over and over again. And after going back and forth for a few days, I finally send her a text.

"Hey Samantha. It's the girl from the streetcar." She calls me right away, another generational giveaway. We end up meeting on Bloor Street that evening. A small restaurant I've never heard of near Yorkville, which I later find out is where Samantha lives.

Red wine for her and white for me. She never takes her eyes off of me. Not once. I don't need an invitation back to her condo. We both know why we had come.

Her place is what I expect. Larger than most of the boxes I've been in. Two rooms even though she lived on her own. No kids, though I feel a bit like a child when she kisses me on my cheek.

Then my neck. Slowly down till she lifts my dress and shifts my panties. It feels like I've stopped breathing. Like my entire body is on fire and if I exhale it would fizzle out. This is the first time I've ever screamed.

It isn't the last time I see Samantha. We're friends, yes, but only in our own created world. We go out only with each other. There is never anyone at her place when I'm over, not even a trace of anyone else. No extra plate in the sink, no shoe that doesn't match, no wet bath towels. It's always just us.

And I like it that way, prefer it the longer we last. Samantha never answers a call while we're together, barely replies to any texts. She treats me like she's here for me only. Actually, more that I think about it, I think I'm here for her.

That kind of attention gets addictive. Messages returned right away, phone calls always answered, invitations never turned down. She takes me to see Gas Light and Kinky Boots. I take her dancing and to the weed cafe in Kensington.

Days pass. Weeks take their place. The thrill is still present, her tongue still magical. I almost tell her I love her. She laughs when I fumble my words. I feel like a child again.

***

JUSTIN

The same dream again. The only difference is this time I see her face. We're close, touching close. I ask her if she's dreaming, too. If she's somewhere laying in her bed and dreaming the same dream. If when she wakes up she still sees me like I still see her. She says she does.

"How can this be?" I ask her. "How can we be dreaming the same dream?"

Neither of us answer, we never answer.

Psychedelic Sundays. I just put out another plate and watch everyone's eyes light up. It's 4:00 a.m. when Steve comes in with a friend I've never seen before. Me and James have been here most of the night, other than the hour we bar hopped through Queen West, which has died down by now, occupied only by the regular nightwalkers. Locals. The 905ers already jumped in their SUVs and packed it up for the night. We're just getting started, or really haven't stopped.

This is going on night two, day three. Weekend binge, doing straights all the way through. Two more people come after Steve and his new friend and add to the plate. A mix of Arcade Fire, Pink Floyd, and Drake keeps the room alive. My apartment is just big enough so it doesn't feel packed. Me and James take the long couch, Steve is standing near the stool in the kitchen, his new friend sitting beside him, watching with eyes green like ancient emeralds.

"Treasure," she answers when I ask her name. "Nice to meet you."

"Nice to meet you, too. Welcome to my apartment."

"Thanks."

"Feel free to indulge in whatever you want," I say.

"Feel free to stop staring," Steve snaps. It sounds playful, but I know him.

And I know myself.

I watch her all night. She smokes a little weed, takes shots of tequila, sips on a glass of pinot, but doesn't take anything off the plate. Everyone offers, but she says no every time, not even a thought.

Psychedelic Sundays. When Jake finally rolls off the couch, it's nearly 8:00am. Two hours pass before my eyes finally close.

I don't dream about her. Not this time. But she's still there, I know because I still feel her in my dream. She's getting closer, we're getting closer. Last time we spoke I kissed her hand, told her she means the world to me. A dream. She was that but so much more.

A shower at 4 o'clock that evening wakes me up. Just barely. A straight when I get dressed really opens my eyes. I sit down and laugh in my head, not because of the girl in my room, but because I'm leading a workshop in two hours and I'm not sure how much I've actually slept. I bend down and take another straight. "That should get me through the workshop," I say out loud.

The summer's off to a wild start. This weekend was the first time you could actually go outside in a t-shirt without goosebumps covering your skin. The cyclists are out, running stop signs and running into more car doors. Joggers are up and down Queen Street till night sets in, and some even after that. And the umbrellas are out. Both for spring rain and patios. Groups of Millennials turning down booths so they can be seen outside.

But that actually only matters to people who live north of Bloor. Living in the city means you don't need reservations to go anywhere, or don't have to wait till Friday evening to fight for seats at the Drake. A Wednesday is just as live as a Saturday, especially when all your friends are bartenders or waitresses.

It's like that scene in Blow when Boston George moves to California and finds out that every girl is a flight attendant. Although these waitresses might not be moving pounds of weed across borders, hustling for tips is nothing to turn your nose at. My ex made 60 grand a year bartending, 80% of that all cash. That's like five grand a month, and you know they're rooming up with someone and paying less than $1000 rent to live in Liberty Village or King West or somewhere on Fleet Street.

Yeah, life just isn't fair sometimes. But who's complaining? Having waitresses and bartenders as friends means the night happens in waves. First cuts come the earliest, that means they're let out from about 9:00 or so. This group catches all the pre-drinking and other indulgences before we actually step out to the bars.

Then the second wave starts. They arrive around midnight, still in time to get some drinks, or sometimes they just meet us at Dog and Bear or Beaconsfield or wherever we end up. This wave just washes their feet and come dressed ready to get right into it. That means rounds of tequila shots and doubles for the first hour.

Then there's the closers, the ones who don't get cut until the kitchen or bar is tapped. It's about 2 or 3 o'clock when they file into my apartment, and their goal is to wind down by turning up. At 3:00 a.m. there isn't much drinking going on. These are alphabet hours. K, M, G, and of course blow is what's being passed around till everyone splits at about 5:00 to do it all again the next night.

"When do you sleep, Justin?" I get asked this question a lot.

"I don't sleep, Steve." True, but not really.

"I know you don't, but you need to. Everyone needs to."

Steve walks a fine line with me. We're friends, best friends, brothers, but he knows there's no lecturing me. So, he asks these questions with a smile on his face even though I know he's genuinely concerned.

"I got six hours this morning," I lie. Steve just keeps smiling.

"How was the workshop?" he asks.

"I don't know. I mean I guess it was good but who knows if anyone actually learned anything. Like how much could you really retain in a single two-hour session?" Steve shrugs. "I've been running these workshops for the past two years and I can't say for sure anyone has learned anything at all."

"So, stop doing it."

"And throw away an extra $500 a month? Not gonna happen."

Two years now as a graphic designer. I started doing the workshops maybe a year after I realized rent wasn't the only expense when you live on your own, especially on Queen Street. One plus den runs me $1500 a month before I put food in my fridge. I don't need cable—couldn't afford it anyways—but need the Internet, and I wasn't about to be one of those house poor hermits. Not with my habits.

I thought about getting a roommate, but that wouldn't work either. I kept imagining the posting:

Looking for roommate for Queen West apartment. Must be OK with drinking, coming home to drugs on the table, all night parties, and loud music at any time of day. Preferably a single female.

A roommate wasn't happening. Running the workshops makes things a little easier. Steve was actually the one who gave me the idea. He lives out on Fort York now and his ex-roommate was doing the same thing. The first one I actually did out of my apartment. Three people showed up. I charged $50 a head and gave everyone bottled water. Not a bad gig, I thought, and I really only needed 10 people to make a good profit.

The thing about me is that I have an actual career that makes me money. That means I'm the exception. Most of my friends, especially my female friends, waitressing and bartending is their job, how they make their money, but it isn't their careers. Almost all of them have something else they want to do. Jenny is a makeup artist interviewing at MAC. Patricia finished OISE and is supply teaching. Tiffany is a painter who just opened her own gallery with another artist who graduated from OCAD. I can go on, trust me.

But everybody gets by. Whether we room up, work 14 or 15 days straight, sell a little weed, we get by. And somehow always find time to end up together for the weekend.

***

She looks so familiar. I want to reach out and touch her face. My eyes shift to each of her movements. They follow her hand through her hair, her chin lifting when she laughs at something she actually thinks is funny, her shoulders when she sips her drink. It's all too familiar.

"Why do you guys call it straights?"

It's the first time Treasure has spoken to me without me asking her some pointless question.

"Straight is just something me and Steve came up with in high school. It was like code when we were on the phone around our parents. If one of us had some blow, we couldn't just come out and say, 'Yo, you wanna do some lines tonight?' So we'd just say 'Let's just keep it straight tonight.' It was funny because even when our parents asked what we'd be doing, we'd say, 'Just keeping it straight tonight, Mom.' The hardest part was doing it without cracking up."

I get a smile.

"So, then everyone just started saying it?"

"All our friends, yeah. It's not like universal Toronto slang, though. What they say out in Valleyfield?"

"Lines. But I like straight, I could get used to it."

"Even though you won't ever do it?"

Treasure just looks away without answering. I keep thinking she probably tried it once and started twitching, or her nose bled for like a day or something. Not many people turn down blow when it's right in front of their face.

I know I never could. Steve would sometimes, or pretend to turn it down before finally saying 'OK, just a couple. But that's it.' An interesting note: Me and Steve are the only ones of our friends who were actually born and raised in Toronto. The rest are all transplants who migrated to the city to go to U of T or Ryerson and just stayed, or just really got tired of the small town life and took the big leap.

One time Steve and I tested out this theory. We pretended we were uni students doing a survey for whatever project we made up. We set up a booth in King West and asked people to answer one simple question: Original place of residence.

About 70% were transplants, and most of them from hours outside the city.

Thunder Bay, Geraldton, Cornwall, Calgary (yes, in Alberta), Midland, Sault Ste. Marie. But all of them managed to find their way to Queen West, or Fort York, or King West, or Kensington, or The Annex. And once they were in Toronto, only a wedding ring could take them away.

I grew up in Ronci. Went to elementary and middle school across the street from my house, then on to private school before taking a year off just to not have to see the inside of a classroom for a while. My parents let me stay in the basement rent free as long as I kept a job.

"And only for a year," they'd said. "Then you either go to school or pay your own way around here."

A final act of generosity before they were taken away from me.

It's a funny thing to have your parents die when you're still young. Funny in the way clowns are funny. You're stuck with this stupid mask painted on your face. You smile and you laugh and you joke, and everyone knows it's just an act. *You* know it's just an act. But you do it long enough till you convince yourself it's real, that you really are OK with your parents being gone before your 20th birthday, like they weren't just robbed of their lives and you'll never see them again.

Then you get tired of the mask. The paint starts chipping away. The colours start getting dull. You don't know what to do, or who to be. So you say fuck it and be whoever the hell you want to be and do whatever you want to do. You realize that there are no rules in this life. Any rule can and has been broken. Everything logical can be made surreal. Every system has its cracks. The only way to live is to learn all the rules so you can shatter them every chance you get.

That year living in my basement when my parents were still alive, I got lucky. I nabbed a job selling merch at concerts and Jays games inside the Rogers Centre. It paid OK, and I got a commission on sales (Hallelujah, Taylor Swift concerts). The best part was actually meeting people. Girls, I should say.

I just stood in my booth with my hair resting near my shoulders, beard that probably looked just as long, and didn't say a word. The word I got called the most was pretty.

"You're so pretty looking," girls would say. Or, "you're better looking than I am?" Like that was supposed to be a compliment. I was never quite sure how to take that. I knew they meant it as some kind of endearment, that I looked good enough to be a girl. I guess that I should've been more receptive. And I was a little bit. I wasn't about to turn down phone numbers from 28-year-olds living in condos on Queens Quay.

So, I didn't. Not one. And that's how I made all my friends and then realized it's not cool at all to be living in your parents' basement. Not when I saw how good it could be on your own. The midday drinks, brunch with four friends on a Tuesday, live band on a Thursday at Rivoli with two friends who know the lead singer. The city could be unreal sometimes. I knew I had to live on my own.

Then my parents passed and I had no choice but to be on my own. Suddenly, the thought didn't seem as exciting. Petrified is the word that comes to mind. For days I wouldn't even leave the basement. I stopped showing up for work without telling my bosses a thing about my parents. I'd just lay on my couch and dream.

These crazy dreams of being at the bottom of a waterfall looking up at the floods of water. But my eyes are closed and my hands are tied behind my back. No matter how intense the pressure, I don't fall, I don't drown, I just take it. The dream always ends with me sitting near a lake, on the bench or in the sand, far away from the waterfall, dry, smiling.

I'd wake up and feel like I'd been suffocated. Like someone gripped their hands around my throat and squeezed and squeezed till I passed out. It would take minutes for me to catch my breath. What's even more frightening is that I'd never wake up on the couch where I fell asleep. I was always curled up in a corner or on the tile in the bathroom.

I thought the funeral would bring some closure. Seeing both parents being lowered into the ground one by one. Me not making any sound, not turning away, watching everyone else throw dirt on each casket while I stood motionless. Acknowledging condolences with my best clown face.

I'd blink and be back at our house, or the house, I'm not sure what to call it anymore.

Soon it wouldn't be anyone's house. Wait, that wasn't true. Soon, another family would call this house home. Another son or daughter who throws their clothes all over the floor. Another mother making phone calls in the study. Another father making chicken burgers from scratch in the backyard every Saturday over the summer. Soon my memories of the place wouldn't occupy any space outside my mind.

"That really fucking sucks," I said to myself.

I waited for my mom to scold me for swearing.

I waited for my dad to fight back laughter when mom is scolding me for swearing.

How am I going to do this?

***

I read Treasure's Facebook post:

"Selling some stuff to make rent. Clothes, makeup, jewelry, and if it really comes down to it, I might even sell a pair of shoes. Just one though so don't get too excited. I'll be around all weekend so drop by whenever you can."

It takes me fifteen minutes to jump in and out of the shower and throw on a pair of denims. Only Treasure and her roommate are there when I get to her condo. The place looks different since the first and only time Steve had me follow him over. They added a small red single seater, some kind of cloth material. And Treasure's laptop is open on the island in the kitchen, so I assume that means the Wi-Fi is finally working.

"I'm not sure you'd like any of my dresses," she says.

"That's OK. I was only here for the makeup."

Treasure offers me a glass of last night's Veuve. Her roommate sticks her head in from the balcony and waves hi.

"How are sales going?"

"Nowhere." Treasure says she was a bit dramatic on her Facebook post and wasn't actually prepared to sell her clothing, so she only showed a few pieces of jewelry and some makeup kits to anyone who came over.

"Grand total of $22."

Treasure doesn't sound upset or even a bit concerned. Even though it's only about a week till the month is over, she doesn't have that panicked look on her face. She's still effortless.

"Cheers to biting off more than you can chew." We touch glasses. "You'll be fine," I say. "The martyr role doesn't suit you too well."

Something so familiar. I just keep staring at her and thinking there's something so familiar. About the way she looks at me from over the wine glass when she's taking a sip. Something about her neck when she turns to the side and pulls her hair back.

Now I'm wondering if she's wondering. Wondering if she knows I'm wondering. Does she realize my glances are too steady, or that we've sat across from each other on stools in her kitchen for going on two hours without a break in conversation? Does she know?

I ask her when Steve gets back.

"I should be asking you," she says.

"I'm guessing some time tomorrow night."

The first pause. Now we avoid meeting each other's gazes. Treasure stands up and opens the fridge, looking for nothing in particular.

"I don't think I've eaten all day."

"Then let's go."

"Go where?"

"Get something to eat. You said you're hungry, so let's grab something to eat."

"I didn't say I was hungry, I said I haven't eaten." She smiles and sits back down, leans over now with her chin between both her palms. "So, you wanna take me out to eat? Is that what you're saying?"

"Yeah, well I mean, if that's OK with you. People do eat sometimes."

"You know if you pay that means it's a date." Playful.

"Think of it more like a reward for all the hard work you put in today. It takes a lot of energy to not sell anything."

We decide on Local in Liberty Village. It's still early enough for us to get a seat on the patio. A burger for both of us and three drinks each and we're back at my apartment.

Everything so familiar.

Everything so silent. How do you make love to someone you've only dreamt about touching? How does the first time you touch feel like the last person you'll ever be with? Wine and tequila may make the sex exciting, but being lost in those emeralds makes that night memorable.

Treasure is already awake with her arm over my chest when I wake up the next morning. Neither of us moves, and it's more than a few minutes before either of us says a word. It isn't any kind of guilt that keeps us quiet. We both know what we did. I knew from the first night she walked into my apartment that nothing would stop me.

And she knew, too. Maybe not as soon as I did, but she knew. There was something always there, always present. Something between us; familiar, overpowering, magnetic, natural. I hate to be cliché but it really feels like we're meant for one another.

Even deeper than that, though. It feels like we had already been together. Laying there in bed, neither of us saying a word, both of us simmering in the other's heat, all of it feels like it should. Like we've already committed to one another, moved in together and decided to start our own family. That kinda deep.

I touch her beauty marks. One by one on her back and the one arm she has over my body. 'So many,' I think.

"Can we stay like this all day?" I say. Treasure smiles without looking over at me.

"I thought that was already a done deal." My turn to smile.

"I figured you had somewhere to be. Didn't want to make any assumptions." That gets her head to pop up.

"Listen. I'm exactly where I want to be right now. And when I do get home, I'll let Steve know that, too." I'm not sure what to say after that. I don't know exactly what the deal was with Treasure and Steve, but I know it was something.

I nod. She's still smiling then rests her head back on my chest.

"I wanna tell you something," Treasure starts. "I got into a car accident a few years ago. Actually, I got hit by a car. My dad tried to push me out of the way but we both ended up getting hit."

"Is he OK?"

"That's a tricky question. He can walk OK, but stays in his wheelchair most of the time and probably still hasn't done much rehab. But he was different person after the accident. You'd have to know him to really get it. But he was just different."

"And what about you? Did the accident leave any scars?"

"No not scars. I actually came out feeling a lot better about myself. And looking much better, too. It changed my life."

"Wow. So, you're telling me getting hit by a car made you look better? What the heck did you look like before?" Treasure pinches my nipple.

"I'm not done yet, though. After the accident, I started having these dreams. Like these really lucid dreams. And they were always the same. There was a boy, and we spoke to each other. Like back and forth like it was real life. Different conversations all the time. And he always asked me if I was dreaming, and I asked him the same thing. We both knew."

***

How do you remember silence? How does the thing you remember most about a night of drunk sex is hearing nothing? But I swear everything was silent. I know it doesn't make any sense, but that's what I remember.

Even though it felt so good to finally have him inside me. To finally feel his weight on top of me. To wrap my legs around his back. To have him stare in my eyes. I must have been moaning. My lips touched his ear. His were on my neck. I must have been screaming but silence is all I remember.

And when I wake up on his chest the next morning, my mind takes me back to the first time we met. Him reaching for my hand and telling me his name was Justin. Me telling him my own name. Steve shadowing.

There was something there even then. Something ironic about the entire scene, familiar even. Like deja vu but more subtle. It wasn't like I'd been inside Justin's house before. But him. He seemed so familiar.

But Steve had brought me there so I kept it cool. I didn't want to be completely disrespectful. They were friends, good friends. And Steve and I were...whatever we were. We were friends, yes. A bit more even. But we weren't actually anything.

I met Steve the end of first semester, the semester I decided I wasn't going back. It was actually my second year in university, but I already knew this wasn't what I wanted. Studying biology in class was one thing, but when I took an internship at Sick Kids my first summer, I knew I couldn't do it.

Seeing people younger than me fighting for their lives every single day. Knowing too many of them wouldn't make it. Knowing even the best doctors in the world could only save some of them, and that the others were terminal. That thought was too much. I went back to school for one more semester, but had already checked out.

Sometimes I think the whole Sick Kids thing was just an excuse, though. A really good one, but an excuse all the same. University was really just a way for me to get out of Valleyfield. A full scholarship meant my parents didn't have to pay for anything, and I could live in the city I've dreamed of since before my accident.

But going to class four times a week for something that never really excited me wasn't going to last. I knew that pretty early on. And when I finally decided I had enough, the city opened up even more.

Plus, being on campus reminded me too much of being in Valleyfield. Everyone belonged to some kind of group, every boy belonged to some girl. I caught myself having to be careful again, almost sneaky about who I hooked up with. Taking those walks to different dorms was like taking those walks to different boys' houses back in high school. And I wasn't about to relive any part of my existence in Valleyfield.

Not here. Not in Toronto. Not now, not ever. I had already started waitressing the semester before I dropped out. I told my manager I could take on more shifts and he gave them to me.

Waitressing was perfect. I saved up enough money for first and last in less than two months once I started getting better shifts. That was huge since I technically shouldn't have been staying in my dorm room, which I was right up until I moved out that April.

But that wasn't the best part. The best part about being a waitress was meeting all these people. I loved it. Without even trying, I got invited to nightclubs, theatres, concerts, private parties. And in most cases I didn't have to pay for anything. Just show up, or I should say just get picked up and go.

Being a waitress also put me in some awkward situations. On more than one occasion, I got called out by girlfriends for being too friendly with their guys. Or that's what they thought. It was my job to be friendly, but they took a flip of my hair at the wrong moment as flirting. Or the way their guy smiled back at me when I introduced myself as me leading them on.

More than anything, though, it was my eyes. I could approach a table straight faced, act like a bitch on day two of her period and still stir up some kind of insecurity from whichever female on the other end of the table is wondering why I'm flirting with her man.

Of course, most of the time it wasn't true. But sometimes. Sometimes it was just way too much fun. And way too easy. Guys can be such dicks, especially when they start thinking with it. And especially when I wanted it.

All it took was an extra smile, a glance or two a moment too long. Some guys would come find me, searching through the restaurant like a little puppy looking for its owner. Sometimes I took their number, but most of the time I politely lied and said "Sorry, but I'm already taken." Just like that, in a pretentious, almost sarcastic tone, then watched them pout on the way back to their seat.

But other guys, the ones I wanted, the ones that looked too delicious to risk not tasting, those were the ones I plotted on. Those were the tables I checked up on one too many times, barely looking at the girlfriends when going over the specials or asking if they wanted dessert.

Those were the ones who left their numbers on napkins or their business cards under plates. Sometimes I got bold and left my own number on the bill, carefully creased and set to his side of the table.

"Is there a reason you're only looking at him?" the girls would ask. Or more directly, "I'm sorry, but I don't appreciate you flirting with my boyfriend/fiancé/husband right in front of my face."

I always apologized, told them there was some kind of miscommunication. "I'm just trying to be friendly," I would object. "I would never intentionally do anything like that."

Sometimes they bought it. Mostly they didn't. That's how I met Steve. He was at my restaurant with a friend, a girl. Grey eyes, straight dark brown hair, cute but nothing special. I couldn't tell if they were together or not. It really didn't matter at all, though. When she got up to go to the bathroom, I walked right up to him.

"Hand me your phone." Steve didn't even flinch. He unlocked his phone and I dialed my number.

"Use it," I told him. "Nights are usually better for me."

But it was an odd thing with Steve. We hooked up a few times, but it always felt more like a friendship. Like a silent agreement that if neither of us had anyone else for the night, we would end up together. And together didn't mean we did anything more than watching a movie in my room, or smoke a joint and pass out on the couch. And neither of us cared if the other slept over, which was normally a no-no, especially for me.

I couldn't say we were together, though. And now here I am laying in his best friend's bed. His best friend underneath me counting the beauty marks on my back. And it all feels so familiar. Scary almost.

"There was a boy, and we spoke to each other," I continue. "Like back and forth like it was real life. Different conversations all the time. And then he always asked me if I was dreaming, and I asked him the same thing. We both knew. We both knew we were dreaming. But we both knew we were two real people. That somewhere we both had our own lives, and that we would each wake up in different homes, on different beds, till the next time we saw each other."

Justin doesn't say anything. For a minute, I think he's fallen back asleep. But he just stands up, calmly. He looks at me, still not saying anything.

"The alcohol finally wear off?" I smile, but I'm being serious.

"Till we dream again."

My turn to stare. "Till we dream again."

Scared now again. Genuinely. Justin starts pacing the room but never takes his eyes off me. I sit up, sheets at my ankles.

"There's no fucking way this is possible." Justin sits at the edge of the bed, close enough so he can put both hands on my face.

"Are we dreaming right now?" I can't answer. "Tell me, are we fucking dreaming?"

He keeps my face in his hands. We stare. In a way, it's still a dream that we were in the same room, same apartment, same city. It's incredible we're living in the same world at the same time.

"It's real." My first words. I hold Justin's wrists. "All of it. It's really real."

His eyes are first to tears. I'm still catching up to the moment. Justin finally pulls away and opens his drawer.

"If this is a dream I shouldn't be able to sniff this. Everything would be perfect. I would wake up right before I put this straw to the plate."

Justin inhales. Deep, hard. He shakes his head and opens his eyes.

***

TREASURE

It's been two weeks since I last spoke to my mom. One missed call and a few text messages back and forth in between. I know she wants me to come home for a while. Summer is close, and it's going on two years since I left Valleyfield.

I'm in love. Not an odd thing to say for someone just over a year removed from her teens. Time doesn't even make sense. Hours pass with us doing nothing. Days pass without us ever leaving the apartment.

Neither of us care.

Neither of us stop staring. Both still in shock, a feeling we hope never leaves us. Feelings neither of us understand, or try to understand. We both know, though. We both know how rare we are. How unlikely we were to collide the way we did.

Twin souls. Justin looked it up. It's actually a thing, or a thought. A concept people want to believe, say they believe, like unicorns and glass slippers. Like soulmates but much deeper.

It actually doesn't even matter. We matter. We matter because we're living it. Us, the two of us. For years we dreamed of each other, spoke to each other in these dreams.

"Till we dream again." That's how we knew. That's how we would end each dream, knowing we would dream again, and speak again. But never once thinking we would ever meet outside of our minds.

But here we are. Like really, here we are. What kind of forces were at work to bring us together? Sometimes I would just cry. Justin didn't mind. He said I was just shining my emeralds. That they needed that every once in awhile so I could see everything more clearly.

We're in love. With each other.

I wonder what Samantha would think. I had told her about my dreams, about the boy and how we grew up together. She had listened without laughing. I'd probed her face for some kind of disbelief, something that said, "This kid is crazy."

But nothing. She'd believed it, or she believed me.

"I think that's incredible," she'd said. And her response was much the same when I told her I found him. That I found Justin, the boy in my dreams. It was over the phone this time so no chance to probe her expression, but I imagined her smiling the way she does.

"Come over," she'd said. And I would, but not for another few weeks. I wanted to soak this up, whatever this was I wanted to remember this feeling forever. Like really forever. Long after we were gone, I wanted my spirit to be able to reflect on this moment and feel this feeling.

My mom wants me home. Just for a while, although she never actually says how long. She had already visited me once on her own. I was still in school then. I took her to Warehouse (she didn't believe me when I told her everything is 5 bucks), we walked through Kensington, ate vegan crepes at Hibiscus.

"How's dad?" I asked.

"The same," she said. "Walking a little more now, but still the same. He says he loves you, and not to jaywalk."

She added that last part in herself, I'm sure. Her last evening in Toronto, we sipped lattes and sat on chairs in the fiction section of Indigo.

"I can't have children," she said. "Your father and I tried for years but it wasn't happening."

I sat and sipped. I felt uncomfortable but imagined how my mother felt revealing this to me. So, I sat and sipped.

"After a few years of trying, we tried something else. Someone else, to be exact. Your dad didn't want to do it. Said we were fine just me and him, but I wanted to be a mother. More than anything, I wanted to be a mother."

"So, you convinced someone to get pregnant for you?"

"It took a lot more planning than that, Treasure. We had to move out of Valleyfield, which meant we had to lie about why we were moving. Then we had to find someone willing to do it, and trustworthy enough to give you back once you were born."

My new birth story. My real birth story. Just as intriguing though I can't say I enjoyed it. Listening to my mother tell me how someone else gave birth to me. No, not enjoyable, but still sipping.

"We found someone, fairly quickly. Got a lawyer to draw up contracts. Did everything we thought we had to do. You were born a year later. No problems."

"Till my accident."

"Yes, until your accident. She wanted to see you. We were supposed to cut ties, all ties. But she contacted us again and again and said she wanted to see you. This went on for years. We always said no, but on that night, I agreed. I told her to meet me at the bar. I didn't know you and your father would be out that same night."

I asked my mom why now. Why she chose to tell me all of this right now. I didn't even care about that woman, that stranger who I'm a part of. I was fine. I had moved on, was still moving on. It looked like my mom had more to say. But sipping was over.

Now she wants me back in Valleyfield. Turns out when she suggested I stay for a while, she meant a month. Like a full 30 days. She says my father needs to see me, that I shouldn't just forget about my life in Valleyfield.

That's such a joke. I had no life in Valleyfield. I spent every night dreaming about getting out. Then moved to Toronto and found everything I was dreaming about, the only place I ever wanted to be with and the only person I ever wanted to be with.

No, going back isn't going to happen. Even as I think about Amanda, think about all the BAGS. She probably has a whole new group of BAGGERS running around, causing trouble, screaming as loud as they could.

I've only spoken to Amanda a couple times since I been here, both times I was still in school. So much has changed.

Now I'm in love. Did I just say that again? Love, love, love. Comes out pretty easy when it's real, when the person you've imagined for years is real. I don't pinch myself. If I am still dreaming, why would I ever want to wake up. We've been blessed with each other, and dreaming or not, here we are.

I moved in. Justin insisted. Said he would find my roommate another roommate and he did. We woke up together, every single morning. Me first usually, staring like he was a newborn, afraid each time he wouldn't be there. But there he was, every morning, mouth open while he slept, breathing quietly.

Then he'd wake up and kiss one of my beauty marks. A different one each morning.

"I need you inside me," I'd whisper. "I need to feel it."

And I did feel it. Every stroke made me drip, little by little till I burst. Those were our mornings, every morning. Sometimes I couldn't wait till he came home. And I didn't. My earliest shift started at 4. I would be outside his workplace by noon in a black dress and nothing else.

The alley was exciting. The bathroom inside his work building was just wild. We really didn't give a fuck, because really, that's all we wanted to do. And we did, again when I came home from closing. On the balcony or on one of the bar stools.

Some nights we just slept on the floor facing the balcony. Justin didn't have any curtains so we could just stare. Sometimes an hour would pass before either of us said anything. Sometimes hours would pass without us moving out of bed.

Justin still had people over during the weekend. The plates were still out and the nights were still long. Waves still arrived through till the morning, though the faces were more familiar now. No new faces, and one old face missing.

I'd be lying if I said it didn't bother me a little bit. Justin told me him and Steve were best friends since high school. But Steve was just another guy for me. A bit more because we'd become friends, too. But to be honest, I didn't care either way. Steve was a disposable part of my life.

But it bothered Justin. He said he should be the one to tell him. And when he did Steve said it was cool. "We didn't really have anything," were his exact words according to Justin. But then text messages went unanswered for hours. Invitations to come by got ignored. The very fact that Justin had to invite Steve over was indication enough.

When Justin confronted Steve about being MIA, he finally admitted he was pissed.

"So, all it takes is a pretty girl, right? The one pretty girl that saw me before she saw you and that's it."

Justin said he tried to explain. That he told Steve it didn't matter what I looked like, that this was different, we were different.

"Go fuck yourself, Justin. You're telling me the fact that she's drop dead gorgeous means nothing? That if she looked like Amy Schumer you would've still gone after her?"

What do you say to that? Really, though, what do you say? How can the way I look *not* be important? How can it not play a role in Justin's decision, in both our decisions? We were attracted to each other before we found out we were twin souls. Had sex before we knew anything.

Me and Justin see it as fate, Steve sees it as me being a slut. Can't argue with either.

I spoke to Steve, too. Not willingly. He came into my restaurant with another girl and sat in my section. There was no getting around it, so as soon as his date excused herself, I cut straight for the table.

"Is it because it's Justin? Because I was fucking other guys while we were cuddling at night. Are you just this upset because it's your best friend?"

"Who said I'm upset?"

"You don't have to say anything. I think it's pretty damn obvious."

"Listen, me and Justin have been friends forever. We were friends when he fell in love with the girl from Brooklyn for two weeks. Friends when he told a one night stand he loved her in the back of a cab. Nothing's gonna change."

He's trying so hard. So fucking hard to pretend. Yeah, all that back-seat stuff is probably true, but that has nothing to do with me and Justin. None of those girls are me, and he's just mad because he knows he'll never have me again. Actually, he's mad because he never really had me. Bitter, bitter, Steve. You remind me of me at 10. Little Stevie looking for some attention. Don't worry little Stevie, one day you'll find the right girl to rub your belly and fill your coffee in the morning.

Justin tried. He really did try. But the worst part is that none of what he said mattered. Steve wouldn't change his mind, and Justin definitely isn't leaving me because he lost a friend, temporarily according to Steve.

"Maybe going to Valleyfield now isn't such a bad idea," Justin says. "Let's blow out of here for a while. I need a change of scenery anyways. Plus, you might as well get the OK from your parents now."

Having Justin come with me to Valleyfield makes the idea a bit more attractive. I'm still not thrilled, but I do want him to meet my parents. It's time, though not very much time had passed at all.

JUSTIN

I've finally convinced Treasure to take me to Valleyfield. She didn't seem too enthusiastic about the whole thing at first, and I started to think that maybe I was pushing too hard. We've only been together through summer breezes. No cool winds have infiltrated yet. Now here I am ready to meet her family.

But it turns out I'm not the problem. Neither is the fact that I want to meet her parents.

"It's like how a transgender person knows they're in the wrong body, but have to live through it till they're able to make a change themselves. That's me in Valleyfield."

I get it. I don't necessarily understand how she feels, but I get what she means. I've been fairly comfortable my entire life, till I wasn't. Till my home didn't feel like home anymore, and then my home wasn't my home anymore. So yeah, I get it.

I was high the first time I told Treasure about my parents. It was the anniversary of their death, the coldest day ever during the coldest winter ever. I stayed up the night before just ripping straights line by line.

"You gonna be OK?" Treasure looked worried. Tell you the truth, I was worried, too. Last anniversary, I locked myself in my apartment and almost didn't make it out. For a week, I let my phone ring out. On the eve of my parents' death, I snuck out and bought some candles. The large, round ones that come in clear glass holders made the most sense. Scentless, white candles.

I placed them side by side on my windowsill and watched them burn all the way down. I sat at the edge of my bed and stayed awake for the whole thing. Straight after straight as the wax turned to liquid. More straights as it kept burning, more guzzles of Hennessy through more and more tears as night turned to morning.

By then, I was almost delusional. My head felt like it was underwater. I was still at the edge of the bed but laying on my back. I thought for a second what it would be like to join them. I wondered what they were doing at that very moment. My thoughts were starting to make sense, too much sense.

This anniversary, I wasn't alone. 11:59. I lit the two candles on my windowsill. Treasure watched.

"I don't even know why I do this," I told Treasure. "I know they're gone, I know I'll never see them again, but I go through this stupid ritual like it means something."

"But it does mean something. People don't do things for no reason, Justin. Just because you don't know your reason doesn't mean it's pointless."

She sat there with me the whole night. She didn't drink, didn't do any blow, didn't say a word till the morning.

"This is the same day I had my accident." My mind was hazy. Treasure glanced over at me for some kind of reaction. I almost got angry. Just the thought of anything else of significance happening on that day pissed me off. Nothing else matters but their death. Nothing else matters but their accident.

Except that Treasure does matter. She so matters. More now than anything.

"This shit is so fucked up. An accident ruined my life but brought you into it. And then people think there's not a God."

Treasure told me a lot about herself that night, too. While my pain came from actual loss, all the animosity she felt growing up came from her own mind. They were all her own thoughts, her own discomfort, her frustration of having to remain in a place she didn't feel fit.

By default, I lived in the city I loved, and the people who surrounded me created the perfect checkmate. I loved it. Loved being around them, enjoyed the groups that filed in and out of my apartment on a weekly basis.

The ones I knew, the few I didn't. The ones who would come for months straight, then disappear just as long before making another unheralded appearance. They all fit, just as I wanted, just as I needed, really.

The conversations during our gatherings would be light, about nothing or no one in particular. Comical stories about run-ins with cops. Reminiscing about being high in front of parents for the first time or asshole ex-boyfriends and slutty ex-girlfriends. The longer the night went, the deeper the stories got, till it got to what I called confession hour.

"I haven't told anyone that story," is usually how the tale would end. Something about sitting in the bathtub with a razor blade, or a parent never once saying "I love you." Both scars just as obvious in those early morning moments, the plate on the table empty by then. Admissions of unfaithfulness, accusations of the same, the telling of the most private thoughts only a drug fueled night could ignite.

My revelations were non-existent. In other words, I didn't tell anybody shit about myself. Not to say I didn't talk, because I did. A lot, sometimes. But I turned into a listener during confession hour. No collar needed and the drugs and alcohol created more of a veil than any booth ever could.

Everyone thinks that having people over three or four times a week means I hate being alone. But I'm actually alone the same amount of time I'm not. I crave those days, even more than I look forward to those wild weekends.

I'm the only person I tell everything to. I'm the only person I trust with my life, or the knowledge of my life, or any of my feelings about anything remotely significant. It's just who I am, who I've always been.

Steve always says that I'm the only person he knows who can talk to someone for hours and not reveal anything about myself. I always looked at it as a positive trait. Something to be proud of.

Was I hiding something? I don't know. Nothing came to mind, nothing serious. I just didn't like anyone feeling like they knew me. All of me. Knew what I really thought, what I was really thinking, how I genuinely felt or what makes me go.

Knowing someone on that level is a big deal. At least I thought so. For some people, it's easy to tell their entire life story to a stranger on a streetcar or at the bar on a Tuesday evening. For me that was impossible.

Meeting Treasure cracked some of those walls. So many times, I caught myself blabbing.

"I read this book the other day. I don't remember what it's called but there's a young girl whose mother leaves her and her father and bolts for California. Leaves for like decades. No letters, no phone calls, no emails, nothing. The girl has to go through therapy throughout high school, but eventually gets herself together. But her life after graduation is, like, nomadic. She just travels from city to city doing odd jobs, usually something to do with farming or the environment. She never settles anywhere, never builds any long-term connections or relationships. She even gets pregnant and doesn't tell the father. She just keeps on moving, not really needing anyone for most of her life."

"So that's what you want? To not need anyone?"

"I'm not saying all that. Just saying there's some kind of freedom to not ever having to live up to anyone's expectations."

"Sounds like fear to me."

"You think so? I don't really think she was scared. She just knew she couldn't completely give herself to anyone. She couldn't love anyone like they might love her."

Treasure didn't say much after that. Girls have this thing where they think everything you say is a reflection of the relationship. You could be talking about eating grapes in Italy and they'll somehow connect it to your feelings for them.

The one unique quality about Treasure is she never stays upset for long. She'll get over stuff in like minutes. Something would bother her for a second, but then she'll be right back to her normal self. No short answers, no turning on her side or pretending "everything is OK." She genuinely gets over stuff as fast as she gets upset.

Another time I caught myself being myself in front of Treasure was watching the Food Network one afternoon. It was a Sunday evening and we were both winding down from the weekend.

It was one of those restaurant shows where the chef comes in and fixes everything. Only this time, the chef wasn't fixing a restaurant. Instead he was at this, like, summer camp for kids with special needs and who've been diagnosed with life threatening diseases. I mean like close to 300 kids a week come to this camp.

I didn't really care about the new stoves he bought, or how he surprised them at the end and donated ten grand. Throughout the episode, though, he would go around and meet some of the kids personally.

He met a young girl who can't digest more than 24 grams of protein a day. What made her entire situation special was that her older sister actually came to the camp with her. They were shooting bows and arrows together.

Another young boy with multiple brain tumors. He takes the chef to this small lake and they go fishing. He actually catches a fish.

Anytime the camp gathered to eat a meal, they would all pound on the tables and sing songs and make wonderful noises.

I cried. With Treasure laying on my chest, I cried. Tears and everything. She didn't say anything, just wiped my tears with her thumbs and lay back down.

***

Valleyfield isn't close. Think going from Toronto to Thunder Bay, and then some. When we finally arrive at the airport, or I should say the closest airport (we still had some driving to do), Treasure's mom is alone.

It's odd because they look nothing alike but are equally as beautiful. It's like comparing the world's natural wonders. Treasure introduces me. Kay ignores my outstretched hand and pulls me in for a hug.

"No need to be all formal with me, Justin."

I call her Kay because that's what she tells me to call her. We drive another hour to her home from the airport listening to a station that only plays 90s music. I was prepared for some kind of questioning during the trip, but she mostly speaks to Treasure.

They love each other. Treasure looks at her mom the way you would if you met your favourite celebrity and they were everything you imagined. And you could tell Kay squeezes Treasure tight. They exchange smiles, laugh out loud, take turns glancing at each other as if they're both trying to keep this moment stuck in their memory.

The Valleyfield sign finally appears and here we are, in the town Treasure despises. We get there in the late evening so everything is dark and quiet. The only light comes from inside of the houses to either side of us.

Tommy is standing at the door, cane in his right hand. He waits for Treasure to run into his chest. He kisses her on the forehead and whispers something that makes her squeeze him even tighter.

A limp handshake is all the greeting I get.

"She must really love you to bring you up here." Tommy says that as he lets go of my hand.

"She does most of the time."

The attention is still on Treasure during dinner. No interrogating me about what I did or my intentions with their daughter. Instead they joke about the shrine in Treasure's room, filled with family pictures and academic awards.

"You know Tommy did all that by himself," Kay says. "Framed the pictures and everything."

"Nothing to brag about, although it is pretty damn good work."

Mouths half filled with food and laughter all the way round the table. "I swear they're usually not this corny," Treasure chimes in.

"We told Amanda you're coming back," Kay says. "She can't wait to see you. She turned that thing you guys were doing with the kids into a full-time thing. It's all she does now."

Treasure smiles but doesn't ask any more questions. The conversation turns to Toronto and my condo, and Treasure mentions the wild parties.

"That's actually how we met," she tells her parents. "Somewhere under all the weed smoke and everything else that's unspeakable, we found each other."

Kay asks if it was love at first sight. I tell her not for Treasure, but for me it definitely was. Treasure smiles. Tommy ends the moment and says there's no sex allowed in Treasure's bedroom.

"But anywhere else and you're fine."

***

Bedtime. Treasure's in her room with the TV on. I'm in the bathroom, no lock on the door. I still take the risk. Just a quick straight laid out on the sink. One more for good measure, till Tommy walks in like he'd been listening on the other side the entire time.

My head flies up, tip of my nose still sparkling white. I get ready to be kicked out, to pack up my bags and told to find my own way home. Tommy closes the door behind him and leans his cane up against it. He picks up the half-rolled bill I dropped on the floor and takes the line right in front of me.

"Put some more down," he tells me. I do as I'm told. He takes another one then hands me the bill. "Don't be shy now," he says. I take one, he takes another before finally opening the door.

I linger in the bathroom a bit longer, high and trying to figure out if I just imagined that whole scene. Treasure's sleeping by the time I get back to the room. I can't. I'm staring at the ceiling. I know I can't tell her about her dad, but I'm sure I don't have to. She makes more sense to me now.

I didn't tell her I brought any blow. I actually promised her I wouldn't. An hour goes by and the ceiling still hasn't moved. I leave the room thinking I could sneak outside for some air, but Tommy is still awake, too, sitting on the couch staring at the screen. He motions me over, tells me put some more out.

I do as I'm told. It feels wrong but I still do it. A couple straights later and it doesn't feel like anything. We talk over the sounds from the TV. He tells me everything. The first time he did any drug, the girls he was with before his wife, then finally finding his wife and giving all those girls up. He talks about Treasure, her birth and her birth mother. How he and Kay struggled with it for years, argued about whether they should ever tell Treasure.

"I always wanted a little girl," he says. "We both did. But Kay...we did the only thing we thought made sense. Now we have this Treasure."

Then the accident. Tommy says everything changed after the accident.

"Things were just different. I mean, I have to say I'm thankful that me and Treasure are alive, but sometimes God just fucks with you."

"What can be better than being alive?" I ask. "Seems like God is on your side to me."

"Yeah it does seem that way, doesn't it?"

Tommy doesn't say anything else, not about the accident anyway. The four nights I stay in Valleyfield, three of them are spent doing blow with Treasure's dad. Treasure's just happy we're bonding, even when I tell her on the second day about what we were really doing when it took me forever to come to bed the night before.

Plus, it's not like all we do is do drugs. Tommy takes me fishing one afternoon, Another time he takes us all out on the sailboat. That same afternoon he throws some game on the grill and we eat some dishes that take me back to my own backyard standing plate-in-hand beside my father.

Treasure's friend Amanda comes over that day. Another attractive female, but more simple looking than Treasure or Kay. They hug and scream for, like, a minute straight when Amanda pops up in the middle of Tommy flipping a sausage.

They stay glued together the rest of the evening, and Amanda comes by again the morning before we leave. They speak about high school stuff, old flings, old adventures. Amanda fills Treasure in about who married who, who has kids now and which of their high school friends had the most abortions. Treasure asked her about bags but I didn't really get what they were talking about. Apparently, Amanda had a lot of them now.

I hate that we have to leave. There's, like, a peacefulness to Valleyfield I've never experienced growing up in Toronto all my life. A pace different than any Caribbean or South American resort, even. It's like a different level of serenity.

Of course, Treasure would disagree. She never felt any kind of peace in Valleyfield. She planned to leave as soon as she was able to recognize where she was. She felt nothing for Valleyfield, only for her parents and, now I realize, probably Amanda.

And that's enough for Treasure. And when I say enough I mean that as literally as possible. I think Treasure has a limited amount of emotion to go around. Like her love really does have a capacity it can't exceed. I like to make myself think that I'm the one who pushed her limit, who made her love spill over just enough that she didn't mind the mess.

I didn't have to imagine too much. All me and Treasure had to do was look at each other and we knew. We both felt it, all the time, without fail. She rested her hand on mine the entire time we were on the plane to Valleyfield, even the hour or so we both slept. she sat on my lap any chance she got; on her parent's couch, at the dinner table before everyone started eating, in the bathroom early in the morning before we went sailing (I told her that was just wrong).

But it felt right, everything did, all the time. The one time we're alone for the entire Valleyfield trip, Treasure takes me on a walk by her high school, which doubled as her elementary and middle school, as well.

"I made this walk like a thousand times," she says. "Most of the time by myself, till my dad bought me my first phone. I hardly spoke to anyone on that thing, just recorded all my thoughts. Anything that was in my head was on that phone."

Treasure says she never erased any of those recordings, just listened to them over and over again in her room.

"When I had my accident, I kept recording in the hospital. That's when I started having the dreams about this boy who was dreaming about me too. And now you're here, right in front of me."

"And now I'm here right in front of you."

"What is all this though? Like for real, have you thought about what this all means? Like thought about the chances of this happening? Of us happening?"

I don't answer.

"You're not even a little bit scared that this is too good to be true?"

"I said I love you to a girl in a cab once," I say. "Actually, it wasn't a cab. I think it was an Uber."

Treasure looks confused but lets me keep talking.

"She was a one night stand, a baddie I picked up from the bar. I told her I loved her before we even got back to my apartment. Then another time I asked a girl to marry me on our first date. Sitting on the patio at the Drake, I asked her to marry me."

"Why are you telling me this, Justin?"

"Because I'm impulsive. I say things in the moment because it feels good or to get a reaction or whatever the reason. I say it, then it's over. The feeling is gone and I'm back to not caring. When I first saw you at my apartment, I wanted to marry you right there and then. I wanted to tell you I loved you and that we should move in together and have babies and all that. But I didn't. I waited. Every day I waited. And every minute that I didn't see you I thought about you. And when I did see you, everything was better. Everything felt right. My world made sense."

We're halfway back to Treasure's parents' house, sitting at the top of a hill at the side of road behind some short buildings. She curls her arms around mine and rests her face on my shoulder.

"I'm not trying to prove anything with you, Treasure. I'm not trying to be smooth or slick or say things that sound really good. I'm just being me. And me is telling me that he loves you. And I'll always feel this way. There's nothing in this world that could ever change that."

Kay is just done cooking when we finally get back. A salmon pasta dish that reminds me of Big Slice back in Toronto. We're leaving the next day, late afternoon to be exact. Kay and Tommy both tell Treasure that she should see her family doctor before she leaves.

Treasure isn't thrilled with the idea, but hasn't been to a doctor since moving to Toronto so she gives in. A full exam, blood and urine samples. The doctor asks Treasure if she gives permission to give her parents the results. Treasure agrees.

***

TREASURE

We wake up to Lana Del Rey. Summertime Sadness, Young and Beautiful, High by the Beach, Sad Girl. One of those frigid end-of-January Toronto days. Actually, the weather today isn't really typical of this winter. We only had one day below zero Celsius in December and didn't get any serious snow till mid-January.

Three missed calls from my parents, two last night and another this morning. I'll get to it. Right now, snuggling under these blankets is all that matters. Justin is gliding his fingers over my beauty marks. I stay still. We're back to front, mine to his. He's more gentle than normal, probably the music, but it feels just as good to have him inside me.

It's been a week since we visited my parents. Justin said he had a good time. Said he bonded with my dad. Not sure how I feel about that since he told me they spent three out of the four nights sniffing coke in the living room. I probably wasn't as upset as Justin thought I'd be because to me that meant my dad was getting back to being himself. Can't say that's a bad thing.

Another missed call. This time I call right back and I'm surprised to hear my dad pick up.

"It's the test results," he says. "They came back and it's not good."

"What does not good mean?" Not good like I have an STD, not good? Or something worse, or maybe not as serious? No more laying down. Covers are off and I'm sitting stiff against the headboard. My hand moves through my hair, back down to my lap. By the time I speak again, I'm spitting fingernails out of my mouth.

I wonder why my mom isn't making this call. Why she isn't on the other end of this phone. My dad goes silent.

"Tell me what it is," I say. "Why are you being so strange?"

He finally says it. "Cancer, Treasure. It's cancer."

Not what I was expecting. I mean how many people my age actually get cancer? My next thought.

"Breast cancer?" I don't know why I say that. Like if the word cancer wasn't enough. Like, if he told me it really was breast cancer that I would feel any different, any better, or maybe worse. Maybe I think I would fit into some kind of group because everyone talks about breast cancer.

"No, Treasure. It's called Myeloma, or Multiple Myeloma. Something to do with the white cells in your bone marrow. It's not fatal or anything right now, but...but we need to do something."

I don't know what to say. I don't say anything. My dad is saying my name over and over again, more urgent each time. I can feel myself getting warm, my eyes filling up. Justin comes back from the bathroom in time to see the first tear slip. He's asking me what's wrong, over and over again till my tears turn into wails.

My dad says nothing is final. They still need to run more tests.

"How soon can you be back in Valleyfield?" he asks.

"There's no fucking way I'm coming back there," I tell him. That's the last place in the world I want to be.

"I get it, but there's not much choice," he says. "They need to take more blood, run more tests. You need to see a specialist."

"There are doctors in Toronto, too. I'll find one for myself, by myself. A family doctor for one."

"I hope you mean for two," Justin says. He's sitting on the floor with me between his legs. He belts his hands around my waist. I've stopped crying. Only silence now. I don't remember ending the call with my dad. The last part of the conversation I remember is him saying something about my mom.

Of course, she couldn't be the one to tell me. No way. She's probably in her room sitting back against the wall doing the same thing I'm doing. Nothing my dad could say would console her, so I'm sure he's just letting her be; leaving her alone to swell her eyes while he tries to figure out the next move.

Now he knows that doesn't include me going back to Valleyfield. Out of the question. Whatever has to be done has to happen with me here in Toronto. Justin agrees, but he would agree with just about anything I say at the moment.

I cry some more. I figure I'm allowed and Justin lets me. We stay home the entire day, then two days after that. Neither of us wants to face it. We speak only in questions and answers, as if the less we talked the slower time would pass.

It doesn't work. Time doesn't slow down. It keeps going, and going; faster the slower we try to make our days. More painful by the minute, more aggravating by the hour. Justin stays beside me. He wakes up and still touches my beauty marks. Different ones each morning.

I wonder now. I try not to but I wonder. My mind flashes back to the recordings on my phone when I was 8. Hours of conversation to myself when no one was listening. I feel Justin trying to get inside me now, trying like it's a normal morning.

My dream right beside me. My own mind dreaming, wandering between time. I told that recorder everything. Now Justin's my recorder, my dream, my reality. Right here inside me, inside my mind, holding my heart as gently as he can. But it didn't matter. My emotions are like snowflakes that no amount of tenderness could keep from dissolving.

"We have to see a doctor, Treasure. We need to fix this."

"Fix this?" Brace yourself. "You think the doctors are going to rotate my tires and give me an oil change. This is not something you fix, Justin. This is something you treat day after day and pray that maybe it goes away. Maybe you can live a normal fucking life."

Justin stays quiet. He nods his head and stays quiet. My heart sinks right away. No apologies though. I don't have the strength to feel sorry for anyone else. He's fine. I think he's fine. It's tough to get too many words out of him since we found out. A lot of stares, distant gazes, a lot of silence.

Maybe he's not OK. Neither of us saw this when we were dreaming of each other for so many years. How could we? I wish I could be inside his thoughts again. Run through his mind end to end just to know everything.

What would I see? Justin loves me. This me. Emerald eyes. Long hair. Beautiful; by accident, yes, but beautiful enough to make pretty girls insecure. Beautiful enough to fracture a life long friendship.

I wonder, though. Then I stop myself.

My doctor. She's seen the results from my blood tests in Valleyfield. She holds it in one hand, my life on a loose white paper. Time creeps into my mind again. We're in her office now, separated by a long, wooden desk in an odd shaped room.

Justin's with me, beside me. Sitting at the edge of his seat. She hasn't looked at us yet. She seems so far away on the other side of that table. I lean back against my chair. Deep breaths. No blinking. I think my eyes are closed.

"Well, like the original diagnosis showed, you have a type of Cancer called Multiple Myeloma. The abnormal plasma cells in your bone marrow are reproducing uncontrollably and this is beginning to affect your healthy blood cells." She pauses and looks up. There's some hesitation.

"Umm, we've found some tumours. Small ones, but they're there. We need to treat those right away."

More silence. No tears yet, but it looks like Justin might burst before I do. He's trying his best though. He doesn't want to show me what we both know, or know is a possibility. The doctor is apologetic without being sorry, like, really sorry. How many times had she brought herself to tell a patient they might not live?

One time or many, either way she was always on the other end. She got to get up, walk away, go to the next room, and tell another patient their tests were fine. Her emotions didn't change in either exchange.

I'm angry. No, that's not true. I feel betrayed first. More than by my own body, but by the universe. The universe who for so long had been on my side. The universe who gave me my beauty, took me away from Valleyfield, made me dream. Then made me meet my dreams.

A universe that gave me my world is taking it away. And for what? I'm living my fate. I'm in love. I'm happy. *This isn't karma*, I think. Then think some more. What is this then? What is this, really?

In the Uber back to our apartment, Justin has no words. I have too many and say none. Instead I think of Samantha. I never told Justin about Samantha. Not for real told him. Maybe on a night we hit the bong a few times I told him about me doing it with a girl, but he doesn't know she's significant.

He doesn't know she actually matters in my life. Especially right now because I need to talk to her. I need her to know what's happening, how I'm sick and nothing can make me feel better.

And maybe she can't either, but my mind thinks she could make a difference. Or at least have something to say, or know when to say nothing at all.

That's a terrible thing to say. I know. Justin. He's more than my soul mate, he's my soul. But I need to be around another female. Not just a sometimes friend that pops up when they want to go out on the weekends. Someone who knows me.

"I'll be back," I tell Justin. I don't even leave the Uber.

"What do you mean? Be back from where?"

"Somewhere. Out somewhere. I just need to be alone, Justin. Please."

Who knows what Justin's thinking. He knows I wouldn't do anything crazy, or thinks I wouldn't do anything crazy, but that doesn't matter. I'm not about staying with him tonight. And that's all he knows for certain.

Samantha lets me cry on her lap. She kisses my cheek. Then she cries too. Peacefully, with just the right amount of emotion.

She wipes my tears and pulls back my hair. She takes off my clothes and walks me to the bath. We sit in the water, no bubbles, me in between her thighs.

More kisses. On my back this time. I let her. Her touch is what I need. I give in.

It's morning when I open my eyes again. Samantha's beside me, awake, close. I don't remember falling asleep, or even coming to the bedroom. The last thing I remember was texting Justin and letting him know I'd be staying here.

"My friend Samantha, Justin. Just for one night."

"I don't even know who Samantha is, or where she lives, or that you even had a friend named Samantha."

"I did mention her. But Justin, I'm good here. Don't worry about it. I love you so much. Just give me this night."

"I'll give you whatever you want, Treasure. Although it doesn't feel like I have much of a choice right now. Just come back home tomorrow."

There's a cup of tea on the side table next to the bed, steam still hovering. Suddenly I feel guilty. Samantha's father had just passed. I picture her doing the same for him, putting tea at the side of his bed. Making sure he was comfortable.

Scary.

"I'm sorry," I say. "I didn't mean to put you through this. I know...I mean it must still be hard for you and here I come with my own shit."

"You're not putting me through anything, Treasure, because you're not going to die. I want you to know that. I want you to really believe that."

No response. Samantha turns my head with both her hands. My emeralds fighting back tears but staring right back at hers, hazel, wide, fearless.

"Say it, Treasure. I want you to say that you're not going to die."

"I'm not," I whisper.

"Say it, Treasure. You're not what?"

"I'm not going to die."

"Say it again."

Tears now.

"I'm not going to die!" And I believe it. In this moment, through screams and sobs and insecurity and fear, Samantha makes me believe I'm not going to die.

Back at home now. Justin is sitting on the couch looking like he hasn't slept a blink. *I love this guy so much,* I think. For that I didn't need any convincing. He didn't say anything when I walked in. He was just waiting.

I sit on his lap, wrap my arms around his neck. Kiss his cheek, then his forehead.

"I'm not going to die."

***

I wish we were still dreaming. I wish I could close my eyes and see Justin in a world that didn't look like this. I can't stand this world. I can't make sense of it. It's like it never wants you to have everything all at once. You can love your friends but hate your home. Love your job but hate your co-workers. You can be in love but be fucking dying.

I want to scream. And I know I'm being a bit melodramatic. I'm not exactly dying, there's just a chance I could die, so I guess I should be thankful, right? I should praise the Lord for giving me even a glimmer of hope. Because things could be worse. But things aren't worse. Everything is good. I'm happy. My parents love Justin and he loves me.

I wish we were still dreaming.

***

I'm still not feeling much different. Physically I mean. Mentally I'm a wreck. I float through my shifts, automate my smiles with new customers, and ask just enough questions so regulars won't try to ask me any.

Those are my evenings. The threat of death planted in the back of my mind while I serve customers with nothing on their mind but the menu or drink specials. At least for those moments, anyways. Who knows what problems they're having? What kind of life or death decisions they have to face while they sit sipping Caesars?

In those moments, my customers are fine. They eat and drink and laugh with their friends and just have a good time. It's admirable. They don't wear any concern on their faces. And although the chances they are facing a fatal disease are slim, I recognize how relative the word "fatal" could be, and how any problem large enough in your own mind can damage an entire life.

But I can't help but to think where those moments were for me? Where my living preoccupied my life. Samantha had given me that. She made me present, and for however brief, she centred my thoughts.

But I need more. Or maybe I need her more often. I still haven't decided who I am in this fight. Justin tells me every morning how strong I am.

"Just the fact that you're not crying everyday is a victory, baby. You're being so strong."

If we were texting I'd find the most sarcastic emoji. Or maybe the one that's laughing so hard tears are popping out of its face. Maybe Justin would catch the irony in that one. Even if it were true, even if I wasn't crying everyday, I'm not sure what that would have to do with me being strong or not.

But it doesn't even matter because it's not true. I cry every single day. First in bed usually right after Justin leaves for work. At my own workplace, I'd run to the bathroom for a bit to get out a good cry. No runny mascara. I stopped wearing that the day my dad called me from Valleyfield.

But if I'm not strong then what am I? Instantly I think I must be weak. The extremes. That makes the most sense.

- ☐ Strong
- ☐ Weak

Check one. Then live there. Whichever I choose would be my path, would determine how people speak to me, determine my mood when I wake up everyday. Strong or weak. Choose one, Treasure.

In the mirror, I say these words out loud, naked before I step into the shower, no mist interrupting my view. I see myself.

"Strong or weak, Treasure? Strong or fucking weak?"

I wait. Wait for some kind of sign, a feeling, some spur of emotion. Nothing. Just me staring back at myself. Where's the power now.

***

JUSTIN

I have no idea what Treasure is thinking. Even worse, I have to be OK with it. I have to be OK with my girlfriend being sick. Or worse, possibly. And I can't fix it. Let me rephrase that, because "this is not something you fix." I can't help her. At least that's what it feels like.

I'm not even sure I know what to do. Like what does helping her even look like? Is it skipping a few days of work so we can lay quietly in bed all day not saying anything to each other? Maybe. Or maybe it's pretending like everything is OK. Like she's not suffering from this disease that could end her life.

So maybe I act normal. Wake up, touch her beauty marks. stroke her hair and tell her she's beautiful while I try fitting it inside. Maybe. But I don't know if anything's working. It's not like she's giving me feedback. Not verbally, anyways. I try reading her body language. Nothing. Which I guess says a lot, but I don't know what that means.

Then this whole Samantha thing. She finally tells me that they're actually friends. That Samantha was not just a one-time curiosity but a real companion. Odd, I think. Not that two girls are friends, a girl and a woman I should say, that's fine. It's just weird she waited this long to tell me.

Like why wouldn't she tell me? It's not like Treasure's into girls like that. And even if she was I'd probably be OK with it. But the first time I hear anything significant about Samantha is when Treasure spends the night at her place. And she didn't really tell me where she was till she came walking inside our place the next morning.

She actually just left me. I got out of the Uber, she didn't. No explanation, no telling me where she's going, just pulls off and leaves. And I have to be OK with this. And I was OK with it. That's a lie. I pretend to be OK with it. I pretend because that's what I think Treasure needs from me.

And then sends a text telling me she was at Samantha's house. I didn't get it. I didn't even remember who Samantha was. Before that she was a blimp. Now she had landed front and centre in our relationship.

"I don't care," I lied the next day. "I just wanted to know where you were so I knew you were OK. I mean not OK, but like not hurt or something like that."

Treasure says she gets it. She doesn't say sorry but her tone is apologetic.

"We have a lot to do," she says. She's still on my lap.

"I know. You ready for it?"

"No." She almost smiles. A playful smile, like the Treasure I'm used to. Like the Treasure of my dreams sitting near the sand at the lake. Or the Treasure standing outside the hospital telling me she'll be fine. That she's beautiful.

That Treasure. With emeralds that would put me in a willful trance and force me to do her bidding. That's actually really funny. Treasure never has to force me to do anything. She never really wants anything from me except for me. And that's easy.

That's Treasure's beauty; she makes everything easy. She makes being with her every single day seem new. Both sides of me are present with Treasure. The side that loves hitting the bars and getting high and being around a bunch of people for days at a time. I didn't feel like I lost any of that by committing to Treasure.

Then the other side of me. The loner side who enjoys watching YouTube videos about the genocide in Rwanda as much as I like watching Game of Thrones. The side that doesn't mind ignoring calls if it means I get to sit on my couch by myself for another day. If it means not saying any words at all for a full 48 hours, other than the conversations in my own mind and the laughter from watching Talladega Nights for the fifth time.

Treasure is the only one who knows both of those sides intimately. She was there for all of the loud moments. There, but never hovering. Never peering at me from the side of her eye waiting for an excuse to spaz out over some inappropriate gesture. She was there for quiet moments, too. Just sitting, not afraid to let that quiet be our company.

And that worked for me. Her subtleness. Her energy. And now this.

I hate this. I know what this is, too. This is God fucking with me. This is God asking me *did you really think it was going to be this easy*? He made me dream about her. Then through some miracle made me find her, made us find each other. We were in love before we ever met, then loved each other for real once we did.

When does that ever happen? But God knows. He knows how special that is and now he's fucking with me. Testing me. I know it. Without ever setting foot inside a church since I was a kid, I know it. You'd think he'd give me a pass with all I'd been through. That he'd say *OK, Justin, you deserve this*. But of course, there's more to it than that. More hurdles, more detours, more obstacles.

It sucks. This sucks. I hate every moment of this. Ignoring calls isn't just reserved for those days I want to be alone anymore. Those days feel like everyday. A couple dry weekends go by and now people are worried about me. Like if I'm sick. Like the world has turned upside down because Justin hasn't been out in a few weekends, hasn't invited anyone over, hasn't really answered any calls.

"Hey Justin, call me back. We're headed down to Queen Street right now. Wanted to stop by and see what you're up to."

"Hey Justin! Say hi to Justin, guys. Hi Justin! We're all at Landing waiting for you. Stop by and bring some stuff."

"What's up, man? Heard you been hiding out. Can't blame you, shit gets boring sometimes. Give me a shout when you get this. Maybe we can catch up or whatever."

It only takes three messages to fill my voicemail. I always leave space for one and delete the oldest recording. Steve is the last one I hear. Before this, I can't even remember the last time I spoke to Steve. Definitely before I went to Valleyfield with Treasure. I don't delete his message, no matter how old it gets.

Then a knock on my door. It's like he was reading my mind. Three more bangs before I even get off of my couch.

"So you are alive." I laugh, not at the joke, but because I'm genuinely excited to see Steve. *How has it been so long*, I think to myself. We've had little spats before, but I don't even understand it.

I pour him a drink and we sit on the stools in my kitchen. No chaser, just two cubes of ice and I watch him reach on top of my fridge to grab a straw.

"What?" he says. "You know I hate drinking without a straw." I laugh, we both do.

"Where's Treasure?," he asks.

"She just left for work a little while ago." He nods his head without really looking at me. He's getting ready to ask me something else, something about why I haven't returned his calls, although at least a dozen of my messages are probably still sitting unanswered in his mailbox.

"She's sick." I just say it. I just say it and it feels like someone lifted a boulder off my chest. Steve stops halfway in his windup and now he's staring right at me.

"She's really sick, and it's probably gonna get worse."

I tell Steve everything. From the blood tests on our last day in Valleyfield, to Treasure leaving me at home one night to be with Samantha, to the last few weeks where both of us are doing the worst job of pretending that our lives haven't totally been rocked.

He listens. I can't even tell if there are tears coming down my face. I'm not even sure I'm really making sense, but I'm also not feeling anything. I don't feel like crying, I don't feel sad, I don't feel angry. Just nothing.

"So, this is real then? She's not just another girl you're fake in love with. This is serious?"

"Of course, this is serious. You think I've been tucked away worrying what the fuck I could do to make this better if she was some kind of fling? We've been serious, Steve. You would've been at my door a long time ago if it wasn't."

"OK, OK, I get it."

I'm standing now, pacing. Steve is still sitting, still taking sips from his straw. He doesn't get it. I can tell he doesn't get it but he's here so I know he cares. He doesn't know what to do either. He doesn't even know what to say.

I tell him I just need him to be here. "We're brothers," I tell him. And he listens, and he hears everything I'm saying. But he doesn't get it.

Two more drinks straight up before he leaves. We're better, better than we've been for months. That's all I can say for now.

Then Treasure gets home. I tell her about Steve. She looks tired, drained. It's like the thought of going to her first round of treatment in a week is present right now, loud, in my face and on hers.

She doesn't admit this of course. These are all still assumptions, guesses, possibilities. But for me they are as true as Treasure's diagnosis. Up till the very day we go in for her surgery to remove the tumours, she hasn't revealed anything.

Days she's still at home when I come home from work, I can tell she's been crying. But she never cries in front of me. I don't get that. Who else does she have to be crying to if not me? Who else is as connected to her if not me? Who else is here, every day, every morning, every night?

I ask her one night, actually I tell her. "I can deal with you crying, Treasure. That's what I'm here for. You don't have to be strong in front of me all the time."

She doesn't answer. Doesn't even try to. We're front to back in bed and we stay that way till she falls asleep, something I haven't been able to do much of since coming back from Valleyfield.

Now it's the day. The first day, her first treatment. Radiation is what the doctor told us, us being Treasure, Tom, Kay, and me of course. The first of nine radiation treatments. We all waited. Before that, we all take turns being cliché.

Tom: "Be strong, sweety. You have no idea how strong you are."

Kay in tears: "I love you so much, Treasure. I know you'll be fine and you'll get through this. We'll be right out here when you get done."

Me: Nothing. Just a hug. She wraps both arms tight around my neck and we hug. She actually breaks a smile, too. A noticeable one. I smile back then grab her face and crash our lips together. And she goes with it, without any kind of hesitation.

When we're done, her eyes stay closed. A bigger smile this time. I know.

TREASURE

Small dots tattooed on my body are my new beauty marks. I couldn't tell you how long the radiation lasts for. It could just as easily be four hours as it could four minutes, each round zapping that much more power away from me. That much more beauty.

When the hum of the machine comes on, I begin my dream. Awake, fully aware, but most definitely dreaming. My own creations, my own off-handed imagination. In these dreams my beauty marks are dancing. Every single one of them in circular formations. They make sounds as they dance, faint sounds like the chatter of newborn babies when they recognize familiar faces.

They dance and danced to the humming, circling in my mind till the humming is over. What's even more crazy is that I start looking forward to these dreams while simultaneously terrified out of my goddamn mind every time I lie down on what, for some reason, they call a bed.

"Beds are for sleeping and sex," I told the doctor the first day of my radiation. I was still feeling bold then. Shaken, yes, but Justin sticking his tongue down my throat gave me some strange kind of confidence.

"This thing is like what aliens use to travel back and forth through time. But a bed? No way." The doctors agreed and from then on we called it the time machine. That was even more perfect once I started the radiation, because time made no sense once that machine turned on.

I also dream about my parents. Not think about them, I dream about them. I know they are standing or sitting right outside the door, but I still dream. Always about my childhood, always about some moment that actually happened or at least happens in those moments under radiation.

I remember when I first started dreaming about Justin. It was right after my accident and my parents thought I was crazy. Well first they thought it was cute, then when I told them about our conversations, then they thought I was crazy.

"Morphine, Treasure. It's just the drug they're using to help with your pain. It's not real."

"Of course, it's not real, Daddy. It's a dream. I never said it was real, just that it felt like it was really happening."

I never did tell them that Justin was the boy in my dreams. I'm not sure why. I just never felt compelled to make that call. Maybe I will one day, but right now, the time machine is all that matters.

In my radiation dreams, I always see both my parents together. And they're always holding hands. Odd, because they never do that in real life. Even my first day coming into radiation, they approached me one by one, separately, each saying what they had to say.

But in my radiation dreams they are inseparable. They move side by side, speak seemingly at the same time, say the same things. No morphine this time. No reasoning. But there shouldn't be any reason behind dreams, right?

People just dream.

And I'm just dreaming. Never about Justin, though. I think we've done enough of that. I worry, though. I think about him and I worry. About how he is dealing with this, about how he pictures me. Like what does he see when he looks at me now? Does he still see me, my emeralds, his Treasure?

His hospital tongue kiss was encouraging, but I'm getting weaker now. Each treatment takes something out of me. There's no more lunch time bathroom fucks at his office, no more PDA at the streetcar stops. None of that.

Am I still beautiful to him? I haven't lost any of my hair and I look pretty much the same at this point, but am I still beautiful? Would he still have seen me standing beside Steve the first day I walked into his apartment? Or run over to my condo when he saw my fake Facebook post?

Questions. All these questions. Maybe Steve was right. Maybe I'll be gone and him and Justin will pick up right where they left off. It's already started. Justin told me he came by the apartment a couple weeks before my first treatment.

"We talked," he said. "It was cool. He kind of just showed up, but it was good to see him. Good timing, I guess."

Of course, I didn't act upset, and I really wasn't. But I couldn't stop myself from thinking Steve would have his friend back one way or another.

"It's good you guys are talking again. I know how close you guys were." That's all I could say.

Justin doesn't say much after that. Neither of us does. I wish I knew what he was thinking. He's trying to be supportive, trying to stay out of my way and not say too much. He still does straights and doesn't tell me. Not like he's hiding it, and I'm sure if I asked him he'd admit it, but he's doing it in private now. Like he doesn't want me to see anything negative.

"I love this guy," I think to myself. I'm back on the time machine. Time warp number five, or six. Doesn't really matter at this point. I throw up after each session, mostly in the bathroom once I get back to our apartment, sometimes in the parking lot of the hospital before I even make it back.

"Just let it all out, Treasure. Mommy's here. Just let it all out." She pulls my hair back, Justin and my dad are close, watching, agitated. They know there's nothing they can do. My dad's leaning on his cane, Justin leans on the rental car which has spatters of whatever I ate that morning.

After one of my sessions, I can tell that both of them were high. Mom knows, too, but doesn't care. Who has time to care about anything else but me right now. Selfish, I know, but warranted, I think.

But is it really? Warranted, I mean. Is my selfishness really warranted? It's been six months since my dad called me with the blood test results. That's like half a dozen rounds of radiation and a bunch of other pills. Both my mom and my dad have flown down for each of those sessions.

I don't know if I'm OK with that. With them taking time off work just to be there while I deal with this treatment. It's not like I'm bedridden. I'm weak but still functional, sick but not that sick, which sounds crazy because I could actually die.

I think the thought of me not making it is what scares them. No, the thought of them not being there and me not making it is what scares them. So, they fly. Stay in a hotel but spend most of the time at our apartment. Buy groceries and cook dinner every night they're here.

They've even met Samantha. Figured there's no use in keeping her a secret anymore. Not like she ever really was, but she was definitely just mine. She wanted to see me, and I didn't want to be at her place looking and feeling like I did, so I invited her over.

First, when it was just me, then Justin came home and she introduced herself.

"Nice to finally meet you," she said.

"Oh, so you're the secret?" Justin just couldn't resist. "Was beginning to think you were a ghost or something Treasure imagined. Maybe a guy ghost."

"No, no, just me. Although I have been accused of acting like a guy on more than one occasion. But there's no bulge down there, I swear."

Cute I thought. And I was glad to see Justin still had his wit. I haven't seen much of that lately, just him trying to bend as far as he possibly could to reach me. And no, I don't mean please me. Reach is the right word. Twin souls, remember? I have to remind myself of that sometimes. Not that I love him, but how much I really love him, and how much he loves me.

Because he does. I know it, my parents see it, Steve felt it, Samantha has been told about it.

They're both chatting away now, Justin and Samantha. Justin just can't shut up. He's in the kitchen pouring drinks, Samantha is sitting on the bar stool, I'm sitting up on the couch just taking it all in.

Samantha looks over at me from time to time. She's as beautiful as I am. I think she's thinking the same thing. How can she be this seductive without saying a word? Her glances give me a bit of a tingle, not much, but just enough for me to know that I can still feel tingles.

It's late in the evening now, my parents replace Justin in the kitchen. Short glasses of whiskey get replaced with tall glasses of red wine. Justin's chatter gets replaced with communal conversation. All the lights are on. Laughter makes it even more bright. It feels like one of my time machine dreams.

An accident. An accident has made this scene beautiful. Near tragedy has made this scene real. I've been in the same position on the couch for most of the evening, aware of what's happening, thankful for it all, still scared out of my mind, but that didn't seem to matter as much. When Justin finally closes the door, I stand up. I walk to the kitchen and grab a plate. He's watching me.

I put the plate on the table.

"I want to feel how you feel." He opens his mouth to say something. Rebuttals maybe. Some kind of lecture, not likely. That's not his style. He was probably ready to say something clever and brush it off. Kiss me on the cheek and carry me off to bed.

"No," I say. "Just...no. I want to feel how you feel, so just put it out and let's do this."

He's still a bit shocked, but he walks to the room and comes back with a bag. He wants to ask if I'm sure. He's pouring some of the bag out on the plate slowly hoping I'd change my mind. He takes a straw from on top of the fridge and cuts it in half.

"Make me one. And not a small one either."

He chuckles. My courage is wearing off so I take the card from him and make one myself.

Inhale. Hard. Long. Exhale.

VOL III

TREASURE

It's the morning after. How is this possible? My life had changed so much over the last eight months. No more working, no more dreaming on the time machine, no more anything. No more anything!

That's how it should've been. There wasn't supposed to be anything else—no more treatments, no more follow ups, no more pills. It should've worked, right? All of this pain, and parents flying from Valleyfield to cry for the weekend, and my boyfriend enduring me not being myself, laying in bed all day, not speaking to him for days sometimes. It should be over.

But the day before, I hear whispers. My mom and my dad are speaking to the doctors. Mom looks like she's the one who's sick. Her hair is up, her eyes are swollen, she's looking away from the one doctor who's doing most of the talking. She shakes her head.

Now dad's turn to look sick. He looks at my mom, who can't face anyone at the moment. He puts one hand over his face, then puts his hand around my mom's waist. She let's her head sink into his chest. The doctor's still speaking.

No one looks at me, but I'm who they're talking about. I don't even want to ask, and no one volunteers any information other than saying they're not sure. "Nothing is for certain..." or "We can't make any predictions." My mom's tears are all the confirmation I need.

But I don't ask. My parents take me back to my apartment where Justin is waiting, or where I thought he would be waiting.

He steps out of the bedroom at the sound of the front door opening. Steve is with him, plus a couple other randoms sitting on the couch. An open, half finished bottle of tequila is on the table beside a barely tapped bottle of Grey Goose.

"Hey Treasure," not Justin, but one of the randoms says hi first. The other random waves hi while she swallows another shot.

Justin trots over and grabs both my hands in both of his. My dad knows he's high, my mom is just too caught off guard by everything to notice, or maybe she does. I can never tell with her.

"I thought we'd liven things up in here, baby. A little drink, a little music. Obviously, you don't have to drink. I mean you can if you want, but I thought it would be cool to have some people over."

Steve is just staring at me. Not maliciously, just staring, wondering what he should say, what his first words to me in months should be. I don't bail him out, but he eventually mumbles hello, then acknowledges my parents, who are still standing at the door.

"I can't do this right now, Justin," I say it in front of everyone even though I know he was leading me to the bedroom.

"But that's the best part. You don't have to do anything, Treasure. Just relax and enjoy the company. No stress, just some good drinks and good conversation. That's it."

"I don't want any drinks. I definitely don't want any conversation. I just...I get it, I really do. I'll just go to the room and you guys can have a good time."

Mom follows me to my room. We leave the door open. Dad stays standing in the living room, though he's moved somewhat away from the front door. He motions with his head for Justin to come over.

"Think you might've missed the mark with this one, buddy."

Mom is ready to get into full tirade so I close the door. A few minutes later I hear the front door open then close. I'm exhausted, but the only thing I can think about was how gorgeous that girl looked, the one with the mouth full of tequila.

Fuck. I say that out loud. My mom asks what's wrong and I just shake my head. *She's fucking perfect*, I think. *Beautiful*. Like I am, or like I was? Now my mind can't stop. Now I'm thinking about Justin in the house alone with that girl. And yes, I know he wasn't alone, but she's the only one that would've mattered to him. The only one he aimed all his clever jokes and glances, just a second too long.

Nope. Not happening.

I've seen her before, in this apartment, but this is the first time I've ever noticed her. The first time she's stood out to me, the first time I really didn't like her. Now I'm wondering why she was even here. Like, what was Justin thinking?

"Really, what were you thinking?" I'm back in the living room now, suddenly a lot more energized. "You thought throwing me a party would make me feel better? That I'd like to come home from treatment and just start downing shots?"

"It wasn't a party, Treasure. Just a few people over. And yes, I thought it would help. I thought if people were around it would make you talk to me. Remember what that's like? Us having a conversation? Actually opening our mouths and speaking to each other?"

"Oh OK, next time I'll tell the doctor to tone down the dosage a little bit so I have enough energy to go home and have a conversation with my boyfriend. I'm sure he'll be open to that."

"Well that was your last treatment so there won't be a next time."

I look at my parents. They're looking at the both of us, doing a good job of not saying anything while their daughter argues with her boyfriend. But after Justin's last comment, their silence looks forced, uncomfortable even. Justin felt it.

"It's your last treatment, right?" Justin directs his question at all of us.

Still nothing, just vague gazes at one another. I had enough. I walk into our room, no slamming the door, just throw myself on the bed like I'd finished a 16-hour shift.

I can hear Justin repeating the question again to my parents. Same "we're not sure" responses the doctors gave me. Then nothing. A chair screeches in the apartment above us. Someone just opened the door to the staircase. But inside our apartment, nothing.

The only light I see when I open my eyes are from the lamp posts. The moon is nowhere to be found, hiding no doubt. Mom is still asleep beside me. Justin and my dad are on the couch. I don't move.

I grab my cell phone and dial her number. I don't know what time it is. Samantha won't care. She answers and I tell her I'm taking an Uber to her condo.

"I'll tell the concierge and leave my door open," she says.

No one is awake when I close the door, but I somehow feel Justin watching me. I remind myself to text him before I get to Samantha's. He'll understand. And if he doesn't, he doesn't.

***

JUSTIN
"At Samantha's probably stay here 4 the day maybe a few days love u."

I already knew where she was going when I saw her leave. I saw her as soon as she opened her eyes. I watched her staring out the window, then watched her throw on some jeans and slip out the door.

I could've said something to make her stay. Tell her she didn't have to go anywhere but here. That this shit is just hard on everyone. That I'm being an asshole and thinking more about how her thing is affecting me.

Yeah, it's become a thing now. No other way to describe it at this point. It's a thing that's square in the middle of our thing, mine and Treasure's. And it's destroying us as methodically as Treasure's disease is destroying her.

Is it my fault? Whatever. What does it really matter anyway. I stare at the text. *What am I supposed to say to this?*

OK Treasure I love you too. I love that when you feel your worst, you run to someone else to make you feel better. Makes me feel great about us. Cheers.

I don't write anything. Tommy is already up grating cheese on the eggs while they're still in the pot. No cane in sight. Kay is sitting on the couch where Tommy was sleeping sipping whatever tea I had in the cupboard. I wait for one of them to ask me where Treasure went till Tommy tells me she sent them a text, too. Makes me feel even more special.

Kay's legs are crossed. She blows her tea before every sip. Her hair is down and it's hard for me to believe she's not Treasure's real mother, or birth mother, whatever the PC terminology is. She's staring, not at me, but she's staring at something.

There's no focus in her eyes. Four slices of bread pop up from the toaster and Tommy puts them on two plates.

"When's the last time you had breakfast?" Tommy asks me. Kay eases back into reality. She breaks a small piece of toast from Tommy's plate before he can even sit down, then stands up abruptly.

"We have to go get her." A mouthful of eggs keeps me from having to answer and Tommy jumps in calmly.

"Treasure told us where she is, Kay. We can call her to see how she's doing, but I don't even think that's the best idea right now. Let's at least give her a few hours."

"I'm not talking about Treasure. We need to go get her birth mother. She's the only one who can help her right now."

Tommy puts down his plate. Kay is pacing now.

"You heard what the doctor said, Tommy. An allogeneic transplant is her best chance. We have to go get her."

Tommy reaches his hand to pull Kay close.

"No! Don't touch me. Don't tell me relax or take it easy or to think this over. This is our daughter's life, Tommy. Our Treasure. I don't care what it takes, we need to find her and bring her here. It's that simple."

Tommy nods his head. He sits back down and picks up his plate. I still haven't said a word.

***

Day 3. Kay and Tommy are back in Valleyfield. I'm still here, Treasure's not. I haven't slept since she snuck away to Samantha's. I binge watch Game of Thrones and Modern Family, taking straights all the way through to keep my eyes open.

Steve came by again after day 1. He brought a bottle of 1800 and we downed it in two episodes. Winter is Coming. Seems appropriate.

Sarah's coming over tonight. Just her. I know Treasure hated seeing her here a few days ago. Girls don't care about other girls unless they feel that other girl is a threat. And Sarah really isn't a threat, but she looks good as hell, so that makes her a threat by default.

And I'll admit I wanted her to be here just to see her. Just to look at her. To watch her fix her hair behind her ear before every shot. To watch her smiling at every drunk slur that came out of my mouth. I could have been in the middle of Wayward and still felt like it was just the two of us.

Tonight, it will be. And no, I don't have any intentions of more than just company. But I know there's something to me wanting her specific company. Just like there's something to her agreeing to come over on her own.

She knows my situation. She knows Treasure and what Treasure is going through. I didn't tell her everything, but I'm sure Steve did. I know because one of the first things she said to me the other night was *I hope everything works out.*

She put her hand on my lap when she said it. Leaned in and spoke softly, like she really meant it. I can still feel her hand on my lap. Or I mean I can still feel how I felt when her hand was on my lap.

Night 3. I managed to get a few hours sleep so I don't look like a complete wreck when Sarah gets here. Twenty minutes on the treadmill downstairs and a shower make all the difference.

I let her in. Yup, that's what I did. I mean, how else can I put it. She's here, Treasure's not. I want to be here for Treasure, she doesn't want the same thing. Or at least that's what it feels like, so here I am.

And there she is. Sarah. Right here, right now. As soon as she walks in the door we both know. As soon as she wraps her arms around my neck and I feel her body, breathe in her scent, we don't let each other go. I stand with my back against the front door holding her waist, her arms still tangled around my neck.

God, she is so beautiful.

Everything about this moment is wrong. But her first kiss makes me close my eyes. It's right next to my lips, so close I could taste hers.

"I brought you something."

Her something is three cards, all still in envelopes. The outside of each has different instructions.

Open this when you're lonely.

Open this when you're having a bad day.

Open this when you want to be happy.

"They're all hand made," she says. I thank her and keep them in my hand. A gift.

Suddenly I can't get Treasure out of my mind. Every hand gesture, the way Sarah tilts her head when she tries to remember something, the way she holds the glass when she pours our wine. It's all Treasure.

But it isn't Treasure. And here I am, with a stranger no less. Stranger not because I don't know her, but because she doesn't know me. Not like Treasure knows me. But she's here, smiling, talking, trying. And I let it happen.

I let her in.

For the night, I let her in. I let her know me, let her touch me, let her pick my brain. She enjoys it, and to some degree, I do too. It feels so good, she feels so good, even if it's temporary. Even when I wake up and she's gone, I know she's taken something.

What that something is, I don't know. But she has it now, and I let her have it. And Treasure's still not back home, still hasn't even called or messaged me since she left. I haven't reached out to her either. I haven't called or texted, but is that really my job? Shouldn't she be the one to get in touch with me? She left. She needed space. So, am I supposed to be the intruder here? Break the silence to show her I care, show her that it's killing me that she's not here. That I get upset someone else can sneak in as easily as she snuck out.

But I saw her, and I'm wondering if Treasure will ever see me again. See me like we saw each other in our dreams. Look at me like she did when she wanted me to jump her.

I open one of the letters from Sarah. The lonely one. Inside is a picture of Steve, her, and me the day Treasure came home with her parents. I didn't even remember that pic till now. Steve had said he couldn't help himself one day and bought a selfie stick. We all clowned him when he pulled it out, but put on our best drunk poses when he took that picture.

Life is better with friends.

Even her handwriting is flawless. I flip the picture over and stare at Sarah some more. *Why does she have to be so beautiful?* Why couldn't she have jacked up teeth or a lazy eye, or something. Something so I wouldn't still be staring at this picture. So, I wouldn't text her asking her to guess which card I opened first.

"The lonely one, of course."

I ask her how she knew, tell her she had a one in three chance so she shouldn't feel to good about her guess.

"I just know you miss me already. And I'm in my bed missing you, too."

She keeps getting deeper. I'm not even trying to stop it anymore. Treasure would be so fucking pissed. Just a thought. Here's another one; I don't know if I care.

That's just anger, though. I know I'm thinking that, but it's not really how I feel. It's just my mind trying to justify my feelings, wanting me to think that the only way to feel anything for Sarah is to be angry at Treasure. It's kind of working, but I won't let it get too far, no further than it's already gone.

We're seeing each other again this evening. Sarah says it must be hard for me to be alone right now. Says she can't imagine what she would do if she was in my situation. Says I'm being strong and shouldn't feel bad for wanting some company.

Every word she says makes me feel worse, but not bad enough to call off our date. And that's exactly what it is. Dinner for two at Nuit, sitting by the window on a breezy summer evening. It's all set up, reservations made, outfit chosen, two straights before I throw on my shoes.

Then the front door opens. Treasure in a plain grey t-shirt with tights almost the same colour. Looks like she went jogging, but that's not Treasure. She's smiling, I think. A nervous kind of smile, guilty kind of smile. I put on my next shoe.

"Guess I caught you on your way out."

"You did."

"Can I ask you where you're going?"

"No, you can't." Treasure looks more at what I'm wearing than at me.

"Are you going to see her?" My first instinct was to blurt out "Who?" but Treasure already knows. Not everything of course, but she knows me and that is enough. I decide not to answer. To instead shake my head and just walk out the door.

Sarah walks in only minutes after I've been seated. I watch her walk to our table. Every step. *How is she even possible?* I stand up and she hugs me the same way she did when she came to my apartment the night before. No kiss this time.

Rye and ginger for me, Chardonnay for her. I just want to get it out, so I tell her Treasure came back home.

"Just right now before I came here," I say. I say it and wait for her reaction, any kind of agitated body movement, or biting of her lip, anything that showed any of this bothered her at all. But nothing. She doesn't even look away.

She nods her head and listens. Asks me how I felt about it, if Treasure and I spoke at all before I came here. She sips her wine and keeps listening. I kept talking, much longer than I should spend talking to a girl I like about the girl I love.

There's no way this is normal. Sarah, I mean. There's no way she's normal. How can she just sit there and listen to this? Listen to me rant about my girlfriend not trusting me to take care of her? Listen to me venting about months of feeling like shit while my girlfriend might actually be dying?

"I'm so fucked up." I actually say that, and Sarah let's me. She tells me I'm more normal than I think, and that there's no right or wrong way to feel. Feelings are just feelings. *We can't do anything about how we feel.* "You're talking to a female. Trust me, I go through this everyday."

More hugs outside of Sarah's condo. I don't want to let her go. She doesn't want me to let her go. But those are just feelings.

TREASURE

I'm actually feeling better now. Not better, exactly. Stronger I should say. Day by day, I feel more and more like myself. Don't ask me where all this energy is coming from. I have no idea, neither do the doctors, and what does it really matter, anyways. Fact is, I feel good.

I do. And it's been weeks since my last session. I should be feeling like shit but I don't. Not physically. Justin, though. Justin, Justin, Justin. Talk about taking this hard. You'd think he was the one that just went through how many months of radiation. You'd think he's the one who needed support all the way through; that his life changed dramatically.

It did a little bit, but only because mine changed forever. So now he punishes me. Because being sick wasn't punishment enough. He expected me to be sick and polite. Sick and unselfish. Sick and still loveable, or caring, or give a damn about whatever the fuck he's going through trying to deal with my sickness.

I sound angry, but I'm really not. I feel good. I don't even know why I feel this good but I do. Justin will come around. As soon as he realizes this thing isn't about him. That none of my actions have anything to do with him. I do what I do so I can get through each day. If that means staying somewhere else for a few days, then so be it.

And yeah, I probably should've checked in, sent a quick text to let him know I'm still thinking about him, that I'm just taking some time. But why? Why do I need to remind of him of that? I didn't do this kind of thing before I was sick, so why should I feel forced to do it now?

But no. He wants explanations. He wants to feel like he's the one helping me get through this. He wants to feel special and let me know he can handle me being sick.

Wait, let me stop. Just for one second let me stop so I don't sound like a complete bitch. Because I am in love with this guy. Still. And I'm lucky he cares enough to want to be the difference. But that's not what I need. Not from him. I just need him to be there when I need someone there.

I know that sounds like stand-by, like I'm kind of treating him like a side piece, or an affair. But I don't see it like that. I'm just trying to feel better. And wherever that leads me, that's where I'll go.

But I know the same goes for him, too. And I know what makes Justin feel better. I feel a burn every time I think about him sitting next to her, or her next to him. A deep burn, like I'm still in that goddamn time machine.

But I'm not that worried. It's more my pride than anything. I know she's just a taste, not a threat. They probably hooked up, and I knew they've been out together. I'll give him a hall pass on this one.

I know I'm the one.

"Back to being beautiful." I'm in the mirror now, getting pretty for no reason. Not overdoing it, though. Not me. I just need to look great always now. Every time Justin walks through that door, I need him to look at me. Look at me like he did when we found each other.

So, I'm back on his lap again when we're on the couch. I'm back staring at him till he jumps me. He's back counting my beauty marks every morning, new ones each sunrise. Some spots he touches tickle. Others make me shake.

"Where have you been?" he says to me one morning. "I missed you so much."

Guys. They say the most insensitive things without even knowing it. I let it slide, though. I have been missing for a while. A lost Treasure if you will. And he's been digging and digging and I've been hiding away in Samantha's tomb.

But I'm here now. And so is Justin. And so are our feelings. Not like they ever left, but it was hard to feel anything other than pain for so many months. Now that pain is gone, and neither of us know how long, and neither of us care how long.

All we care about is that the pain is gone, or on hold. Doctors are saying that everything looks good for now, but that I'll eventually need more surgery. Serious surgery. The only word I hear is eventually, which means not now. So, I don't think about it.

I think about Justin, and how he's thinking about me. Only me. I can feel it. I can hear it in the way he talks to me, the way he says "Treasure" like that's exactly what I am. And that is exactly what I am, and who I am. I knew that, but now that awareness means more to me than ever before.

But there's a problem. Samantha. Not a problem like she's purposely stirring up trouble, I just can't help myself when I'm around her. And even when I'm not around her I want to be. Like she's holding some part of me hostage and dangling it subliminally in my mind.

I can't call it temptation because it's not. It's deeper than that. Somewhere between love and lust. A white cloud floating below a blue sky. That's us. And I'm starting to feel guilty so that means there's something there that shouldn't be. But she means too much to me to just give her up because of some asinine feeling from Justin.

"What are you thinking about?" Justin catches me blank staring. "You good?"

"We should all hang out one day." I'm still wondering if that's a good idea as I say it. "Me, you, and Samantha. We should hang out. You'd really like her."

We're laying in bed. Justin found some new beauty marks on my toes.

"That sounds like a cool idea."

"Really? OK perfect. I'll set up a date. You up to venturing off of Queen Street for a while? I know Bloor is kind of a trip for you."

Justin grabs my ankles and starts tickling my feet. So annoying. Even more annoying is that I can't stop laughing. I'm telling him stop but I can't stop laughing. Finally, I just give in. Laughter is the only thing harder to fight than tears. Now the duvet is on the floor. Justin's hands are up my shirt.

This is that love.

A love I can only have with Justin. This is what he missed, what I missed, what I thought for a second might be in trouble. It's so much easier to admit that now that everything's good. Now that those moments of fear are gone. Pretending isn't hard when you don't have to do it.

And I don't.

***

A quiet drizzle on a late Monday afternoon. It's just me at home, till I hear the key turn in the door. I'm up ready to pounce on Justin till I realize it's not Justin.

"Oh." I try to sound as disappointed as possible. "Why are you here?"

Steve. I'm still not sure about him. And despite everything Justin and I have been through, he's probably still not sure about me, either. But if I'm not pretending for myself, I'm certainly not pretending for him.

"And why do you have the keys to our apartment?"

"You mean Justin's apartment." He's smiling. He said it like it was supposed to be a joke, but I know Steve. It's shade.

He says he met Justin at his workplace and they took the streetcar back here. Justin wanted to go to the grocery store and told Steve to just head upstairs.

"He said we should bond." Bullshit! Although in some sideways kind of way, I think that's what Justin actually intended. Maybe not full on bonding, but some kind of resolution. Wasn't happening though, and that's not just because I didn't care to.

Every time Steve asks me a question there was something else to it.

I heard you're feeling better now. That must have been quite a scare.

I think it's odd he's sitting on the same couch as me.

How bad was it? Were you close to, like, you know...?

I'm trying to figure out why he would voluntarily come upstairs when he knew I was here. We're not friends.

Justin must have been taking things really hard. Is it still hard for him? And for you?

He's staring at me now. How did he get this close? Close enough that I could hear him breathing through his nose. Close enough for him to lift my chin with his hand and then kiss me.

It takes me a second too long to pull away. He's smiling like this is a victory.

"Get the fuck away from me." He tries to look surprised. "Is that your master plan? Try to hook up with me so you can have your bestie back. Tell him how I'm a ho just like all the other pretty girls he's hooked up with?"

He tells me to take it easy. Says he's not sure what got into him, that he won't tell Justin.

"Neither of us should," he says. Then he insists he couldn't help himself. That he missed me, all this time he missed me.

"What are you talking about, Steve. You hate me."

"No, Treasure, I don't."

I don't sleep that night. I need to tell Justin. Just say it, Treasure. *Your best friend Steve is a creep.* Maybe not a creep, but he's something.

Why haven't I told Justin yet? I know he'd cut Steve out in a heartbeat. He's done it before, but that's not what I want. I mean that's not what I should want. I need Justin to be good, and he's better with Steve in his life. But am I going to have to deal with this guy coming on to me every time we're in the room alone together for more than two minutes?

This is small town pretty girl problems, only we're in a big city and I'm a beautiful woman. Really isn't anything new, to be honest. I've been on the other side of this plenty of times where I was Steve. Where I was the one luring my friend's boyfriend, getting close enough just to see if he'll take a whiff.

Don't do this Treasure. Do not do this. I'm repeating that in my head while Justin's passed out. It's not like I'm feeling super tempted, I just feel the need to keep reminding myself, over and over till I fall asleep.

I wake up and still can't believe it. I'm thinking of how Justin came through the door just after Steve said he doesn't hate me. How we all smoked a joint and picked up a box of King Slice. I held on to Justin tight for the short walk, made out with him in the elevator, sat on his lap when we came back to the apartment. I still didn't feel better.

I actually felt a bit dirty, and that got me excited. Like aroused excited and I couldn't help it.

I'm so messed up. I thought that the entire time I was on top of Justin and it made me crazy. By now I know I'm not going to tell Justin. But that isn't what's was bothering me anymore. What makes me cringe is getting real with myself. Like really, really squeezing my brain to figure out if I had let this happen and if I really did let this happen, then why.

Why would I let someone I don't even like even get close enough to kiss me? I know what Steve feels like so that could've been part of it. Familiarity, almost like muscle memory. But that's not it, that couldn't be it. Maybe I let him kiss me because I remember what it felt like to be with him more than a year ago? Hell no!

But if not that, then what?

I can't do it anymore. I shove those thoughts to the side and leave them there. Steve isn't worth another minute of my time. I know how to handle guys like him. I'm a bit out of practice, but I know.

"You remember we have plans with Samantha tonight?" I reminded Justin over a banana and avocado smoothie. The secret is a tablespoon of honey and to only use half an avocado.

"How can I forget?"

Justin convinces me to have Samantha come to the apartment instead of going to hers, which means we're ordering, of course. Samantha brings a bottle of red I've never even heard of. Justin and I crack a bottle of Romantico. Both bottles are done before we all make our way to the couch.

Tame Impala, Currents album. *Eventually, New Me Same Old Mistakes*. New classics.

Even Samantha knows some of the songs. She stands up and dances with a glass still in her hand. Of course, I can't resist.

I have to put my glass down, though. Samantha does also. She needs both her hands folded around my neck. It feels a little strange knowing Justin is watching. He's already made two trips to the bedroom. Now he just sits and sips a quarter glass of gin straight up.

And watches us. It doesn't take God to know what he's thinking. Samantha whispers in my ear everything she's thinking. Everything she wants to do to me. She mouths it slowly, brushing her lips on my lobe with every syllable.

I don't even have to imagine. I can feel it, all of it. Every insinuated action. Every sensual detail. Every word she says arouses more heat. Verbal stimulation. Sounds like the title of a new Weeknd album.

Justin is still just watching. Still probably unsure of how far this will go. The dancing is over now. Samantha and I sit touching on the couch away from Justin.

"What are you thinking over there?" Samantha plays with the tips of my hair when she asks Justin.

Too loaded of a question. What isn't he thinking would be easier to answer. Justin still says nothing. He nods his head and holds his glass. For once I can't read him, can't tell if he's enjoying this or secretly hating me for letting someone else get this close.

A caress on my shoulder. Samantha's fingers tracing the spaces between my beauty marks. Me getting weaker. I imagine us in the bathtub at her condo, my hair up, no one else there to see us, or judge us, or interrupt that moment.

The straps on my bra loosen. Justin heads for the bedroom. I'm lost. Samantha won't stop, I don't let her. Tame Impala still playing, *New Me Same Old Mistakes*. Feels like it's on repeat.

I jump awake. It's light outside and I'm still laying on the couch. No, I'm laying on Samantha. I stumble over to the bedroom but Justin's already gone. *Did he come back to the couch last night?*

I struggle to remember. I don't think he did. Shit, he definitely didn't. A slight panic sets in. I sit on the bed and feel like screaming, then grab the pillow and just wail it out.

"I'm guessing he's not here." Samantha's in the bedroom doorway.

"I think I fucked up. I don't know, maybe I didn't, but I'm pretty sure I did."

"How bad?"

"I don't know. What does it matter. Bad is bad at this point."

Samantha lingers. She knows sorry won't help, and hearing it will probably get me more pissed off. Then I sit up to see her in her jade bra and panties. The thought crosses my mind. It's been on hers.

"We better not," she says. "Call me once the dust settles."

She leaves. I stay face-planted on the bed till I hear the front door open again. I peek around the corner in time to see Justin settle in the same spot on the couch Samantha and I had spent the night.

He kicks his feet up and jumps on his cell. Scrolling, humming, scrolling, mumbling, sneaking peeks out of the corner of his eye. I sit sideways on both his legs.

"Hi, Justin."

He says hi and keeps scrolling.

"Why aren't you at work?"

"It's Saturday," he says, still staring at his phone. *Saturday*? I must still be drunk. "I need to get up." He's finally looking right at me. I keep my emeralds wide open.

"So, get up," I say. He gives a meek attempt and then drops back on the couch.

"Treasure."

I bat my lashes a few times. "What? I'm not that heavy. If you want me off, get me off." He's trying his best not to indulge, but I already see his gaze softening, the side of his lips curling while he's forcing himself to be as serious as possible. One more push.

"I'll give you a hall pass. One night to do whatever you want with whoever you want. No need to tell, no questions will be asked."

He's thinking about it.

"Anyone?"

"Yup, even that little cute girl that you like." I couldn't resist.

"OK. And what if that whoever is you?"

"Is it me?"

"Treasure, it's always been you."

***

My parents tell me it's already time to pull out the winter jackets in Valleyfield. Mid-October flurries stage the town in white, but it's the wind causing the real chill. My dad sends me a picture through text of him and Mom, both their hair sprinkled with tiny flakes captured perfectly by a gust of breeze.

A perfect picture. Life seems that way, too. Perfect may be too far a stretch, but it's close. My mom still asks me everyday how I'm feeling, so does my dad, both in separate messages. "Fine" is my standard response, but lately I've said things like "Amazing" and "Couldn't be better."

The texts this morning are different.

"We found her!!!" I can picture both of them sitting in the car counting down when to press send simultaneously.

I'm not sure how to respond. A smiley face should do, which could really mean anything. They can't resist calling, though. I'm on speaker. Mom is sobbing, Dad sounds like he's fighting tears, also. I should be more excited.

I should be, but all of this is a reminder of what's not perfect, or not amazing, or not even fine. Maybe a bit of living in ignorance on my part, but is it really ignorance if I know I'm being ignorant? If I know I'm purposely choosing to live in a state that ignores my illness?

Maybe not exactly ignore it, but not let it control my life, or the thought of it control my life. I know there's a reality I should be facing: facts, stats, odds, likelihoods. Reality. I get it. But my reality right now feels much better than that, much more optimistic, and a lot more fun. There are no maybes in my reality. No percentages or chances. Just people I believe in and people who believe in me. What are the odds of that?

But this morning is different. This morning is all about fighting the maybes and the what ifs.

"She's coming to Valleyfield tomorrow." My mom's voice. I barely understand what she's saying. Justin's awake now but doesn't know what's going on. I'm sitting up against the headboard. He rests his face on my lap and makes some strange morning groaning noises.

"Does she know?" My first question.

"Not everything. She knows it's important and she knows it's about you." My dad now. "We told her it's best to talk face to face, that it's too serious to discuss over the phone."

"And what if she comes and doesn't want to do it?"

"She's doing it." Mom now, more aggressive than her tears would suggest. I can see her closing her eyes and taking a breath before she goes on. "She'll do it, Treasure. Don't you worry about that."

Now I close my eyes. Justin's snoring again. I'm silent. Not my mind though, can't shut that off right now. It's firing thoughts in all directions. Everything's game. Everything that seems possible is flanked by something that seems catastrophic.

"Treasure?" Both voices. No answer, just thoughts with my eyes still closed. "Treasure?" Why this again. I was fine, I am fine, I don't need this. "Honey?" Get over it, Treasure. This is life. I just hate the thought of Justin having to see me with tubes coming out of my face. There's no beauty in that.

"I'm here," I finally say. "So, what happens now?"

"Nothing. Well, you don't have to do anything. We'll speak to her tomorrow and let you know how it goes."

A day spent waiting. How is anyone supposed to live like this? Just like that I'm in the doctor's office again. Just like that I'm back in the hospital. Just like that, I'm laying in the middle of the street.

Then tubes and beeping noises. The sound of my mother's voice, her hand counting my beauty marks. Just like that I see it all again, can almost feel it. Can almost feel the needle injected into the veins in my forearm. The smell of steel and sanitizer. More voices. Speaking over me but to each other. All this while Justin is still snoring.

All this on a morning meant for cuddling followed by an afternoon of smoking joints on the couch. The day has shifted, much like my mind has shifted. Everything is ugly again. I feel ugly again. Justin's head on my lap feels wrong, like he doesn't mean it. Like he's just pretending or buying time till he finds *her*.

Her. Anyone, or that specific her. Doesn't really matter. What matters is...

What matters is I snap the fuck out of this. I'm not doing this again. I'm not going through this self sympathy thing. No way. Been there, hated it, not doing it again.

When Justin wakes up, I'm already applying eye shadow.

"You going somewhere?"

"Nope, we're going somewhere." He gets it. Without saying another word, Justin's in the shower and ready to go before I'm done with my blush. We're out the door, nowhere to go but still going. He doesn't care that we're just walking, not saying much. He laughs when I jump on his back and stay on for ten minutes. Then he veers off into an alley and spins me up against a wall.

This guy. Only this guy. The day has shifted, like my mind has shifted. I knew.

JUSTIN

Treasure's gone. Not like that. She's in Valleyfield. Been there for a few days now. A few long days. Work is the only reason I couldn't go. I've taken more than my share of vacation time, not to mention cancelling most of my workshops. Money matters sometimes, and this is one of those times.

Plus, I don't think it would've made sense for me to be on this trip, anyways. Some things are too personal even for boyfriends. Treasure seeing her birth mother for the first time definitely qualifies.

She seemed OK before she left. Wasn't talking more or less than normal. Didn't seem too spaced out or anxious. It was like nothing life changing was about to happen, and I think that worried me more than if she would show some sign that this meant something.

Not just meeting her birth mother. She was over that before we ever met. But the whole thing with her being sick, with her parents finding her birth mother after all these years. Finding her again I should say. None of it seemed to mean anything to Treasure. She had a flight to catch.

And that's fine. There's no right or wrong way to handle this type of emotional chaos. And really, I should be thankful because Treasure keeping it together means our relationship gets to flourish again. It's really all her. Dictating it all. Somehow making things simple again, making us simple again.

Except there's this small change. Maybe too small to even call a change. It's a shift, barely noticeable, but very much present. A slight note in her tone, how she can look at me for seconds and seconds straight while we speak to each other. I admired Treasure before any of this started revealing itself, but this made me respect her on a whole new level.

Then she calls. That same tone. I can feel it through the phone even though she's hundreds of miles away.

"I met her," she says. Then says nothing. So, I don't say anything. I wait for her to speak again.

"Like, we sat down face to face. It was…. I don't know if I can even describe it."

"So, is she gonna do it?" I was more interested in the part where she says she'll do the transplant or transfusion or whatever rather than the whole reunion thing. Treasure laughs, like, belly laughs.

"No. No, she's not."

***

Treasure's flight should be here any minute. Has it been days already? I must've left the house since that conversation, right? There's no way I can still be in the same position on the same couch for more than a day. That's not possible, is it?

Is it?

Where am I now? This whole thing is more than any Millennial should be forced to deal with. I just want a girlfriend. A normal girlfriend with normal boyfriend-girlfriend problems. I want us to fight about me not answering my phone when I'm out late, or having people over too often. I want her to force me to go see the cherry blossoms in High Park, or me force her to go indoor skydiving, or eat at that restaurant where you have to take off your shoes. Is that too much to ask? Is it selfish of me not to want to deal with any of this ever again?

I already know the answer to that question. I wonder what Treasure would think to know that I'm even asking it. In my own mind of course, although the thought of telling her when she gets off the plane does seem tempting. But that would be cruel, right? Tell the girl I love that I'm leaving her because I don't know how long she'll be sick. Karma would have no mercy.

"Just landed!" A text from Treasure, just like that with the exclamation mark. I'm not sure what there is to be excited about, other than she made it back to Toronto in one piece. I really don't get her sometimes. Is she pretending? Like is she putting on this gigantic front to make herself feel better? To make me feel better? Because really, I don't need all that.

I don't need any of it, to be honest. I just need my girlfriend back, my real girlfriend. The one I've known since before I've known myself. The girl who saw me best when her eyes were closed. Who years later found me in a haze of cocaine and alcohol and parties and girls and still let me in.

And now. Now I'm dreading seeing her walk through that door. I can already see myself putting on a fake smile, speaking in a fake concerned tone, closing my eyes when I kiss her, not out of ritual, but so my mind can wander even for a few seconds.

And when she comes home that's exactly what I do, rather easily I hate to admit. I'm watching myself hold her close. I see my hands on her hips, see me smiling and hear myself letting her know that I'm still here for her.

"I'm here as long as you are, baby." A bit cryptic, but Treasure doesn't even blink. Her own smiles are polite, sometimes they may even be genuine. It doesn't matter anymore at this point. We're both in places we don't want to be and dealing with it. I should say trying to deal with it.

TREASURE

Treasure, Treasure, Treasure. You should've known better. Known better than to ever get excited even for one second that this woman who you've never met would do you a favour. Like how did my parents even approach her?

"Hey, so we know we just used you to have our baby, then banned you from ever seeing her again, but if you don't mind, can you give up part of your body to save her life? We'd appreciate it, thanks."

You should've seen my mother's face when she said no. She was right beside me, of course, her and my father. No way they were letting me see this woman by myself. No way they were taking any chances of anything going slightly wrong. They were too close, I was too close, though I actually never felt that way.

"Excuse me?" My mom stuttering, wondering if she heard the correct words. "What do you mean 'no'?"

The woman, my other mother, didn't actually say no. Her exact words were "I'm not doing it." Dad didn't say anything. Didn't even look surprised. His eyes were as cold as the day of my accident. But she doesn't even flinch, even though her own eyes are full enough to burst.

She cares. Everyone sitting at that table inside the cafe knew she cared, but none of us saw this happening. Even in my anger and hesitation and doubt since my parents announced that they found her, when I finally sat opposite this woman, her face looking like my face, her eyes just as much of a treasure, even I for a moment thought she would say yes.

When we first walked into the cafe, she was already there seated uncomfortably with both hands beneath the table. My parents flanked me on either side and we must've looked mobbish when we came through the door. This woman didn't stand up when she saw me. Didn't even look at me till I sat down, still in the middle of Mom and Dad.

She was alone on her side of the table, but the whole power in numbers thing didn't really apply here. There she was, this woman who held my life in her hands, the same woman who gave me life and whom I had never formally met, sitting right in front of me finally catching my eye. There's absolutely nothing in the world that compares to the feeling of that first gaze.

Her hands were still beneath the table, till she had to cover her mouth to hide her gasp. That first moment hit her too, and her emotions were on the brink of betraying her. But they didn't. Any poker face she had was gone, but maybe that was the bluff. Not one tear slipped. And when she removed her palms from her mouth at the site of me sitting down, she was smiling.

"You look a lot like me," were my first words. She said it should be the opposite. Nothing yet from Mom or Dad. Me and her continued our convo uninterrupted for minutes. Nothing about the past, instead we spoke in the same tone, questions like "Do you always wear your hair like that?" and comments like "I really like your sweater. I bought one just like that the other day, except it was red."

Then the break. The pause we wanted to avoid but knew was inevitable. Neither of us could face the other in this moment, and before the next scene transpired, I was touched by a bit of compassion. I'm not sure why, and maybe compassion is the wrong word, but it was there, some kind of connection, and then the rejection.

"Sorry, but I'm not doing it." Those words floated in the air and stayed there. But my mother would never let it cross the table without a fight.

"We need this," she pleaded. "Treasure needs this. She can die."

"And now you want me to care, right? Is that it?" She said that more calmly than her disposition suggested. "I tried to be part of her life. A small part. You didn't want that, Kay, remember? Neither of you did."

My dad still hadn't said a word. Strange even for him to be this quiet, especially at a time like this when you'd think he'd say anything for his Treasure.

"And you. I bet you haven't even told them yet, have you?" The question was directed squarely at my father. His agitation was front and center now. He chewed his lip, looked every direction he could except at any of us, yet all of us turned our attention on him.

"You think all of this is an accident?" my mother and I were the focus this time. "You think he found me so many years ago by accident?" More anxious movements from my father. "You think I got pregnant *after* you found me?"

And then we waited for something to be destroyed. God only knows which one it would be first.

"You dragged me out of that bar by my hair, Tommy. And that was nothing compared to how much you hurt me when you asked me to give up my child, our child, so you could make your wife happy."

My mom sat still on the inside of the booth. If this had cut her, only a small wound showed, though how deep we'd find out later. She had come to save my life, and not even new revelations of how my life came to be would stop her from trying.

"Treasure can die. Do you understand that? She can die. And if you think I'm going to let some affair from 20 years ago stop me from doing anything I can to save my daughter's life, then you really don't know what it's like to be a mother."

"And whose fault is that?"

"I don't give a damn whose fault it is." Heads from the cafe start turning. Our server stayed away from our table. "We're here right now. All of us. And the only one of us that actually matters is Treasure. So, get that animosity out of your heart and do the right thing."

That's about all my mother could take. She stood up, told the woman she'd be calling her in the morning and that she hoped she would have changed her mind by then. Me and my dad stood to let my mother through, then followed her out without so much as a glance at the other side of the table. I couldn't help looking back, though. And she couldn't help looking up at me. We stared at each other like we were sharing the same thoughts. And who knows, maybe we were. That conversation would have to wait, and apparently, so would I.

***

No one sleeps that night. Not even close. Mom and dad don't even speak, or I should say my mom doesn't say a word to my dad. And from what I see, dad isn't exactly trying to spark any convo, either.

There's just too much shit going on all at once. Too many problems to address, too many questions no one wants to ask, and too much junk behind those questions with too much at stake to deal with it all in one day. And because my problem is theoretically life or death, guess who gets all the attention. Deserved, maybe. Probably. But I'm ready to get back to living my life, and that isn't gonna happen in Valleyfield.

Not in this town. Not possible. No way. I needed to get out. Justin being in Valleyfield with me last time I was here distracted me from how much I actually despise this place. No, that's not true. I don't hate Valleyfield, just hated living here. Something about it was like trying to digest raw chicken.

And I couldn't shake it, no matter what I did I couldn't shake that feeling. More family comes over to the house after our first duel with my birth mother. Her name is Chloe, by the way. For some reason, I don't believe that's her real name. Not her real first name, anyways. Maybe her middle name or a pet name or something like that. She just doesn't look like a Chloe.

I avoided ever saying her name for good reason. And when we first saw each other, I had this strange compulsion to call her mother. As a kind of joke, of course. I juggled the idea in my mind for a bit then chickened out as soon as we walked in the cafe. Just an hour later and here I am with aunts and cousins and uncles all sitting or standing at my parent's home. All of them taking turns sneaking glances to see if my sickness is visible.

There's something so pathetic about sympathy. I can't stand it. I mean, I get empathy, but sympathy? I don't see the point. As I get passed around the room, I wonder to myself if I've always felt this way. If my hatred for people feeling sorry for other people was new, or if it was already ingrained.

What does it matter at this point? Here I am, front and center. No, that's not even true. Here my disease was, front and center. There was really nothing special about me having the disease. You could've replaced me with any one of my family members and everyone would have gathered and reacted in the same way. I'm incidental.

And that sucks. To think that none of these people are actually coming just to see me. That just me being back in Valleyfield wasn't enough to warrant a full family reunion. Never mind I rarely come back to visit, or that I've been able to forge a life for myself in Toronto without any help from any of them. Forget all that.

Doesn't mean anything, right? Not to any of them. But they're family so I play along. Tell them I feel fine, that I really am not feeling many symptoms. The gilding is exhausting, but I'm good at it now, better than I should be. And that's what they want to hear, anyways. My Aunt Sylvie doesn't want me to say, "I feel like shit." My Uncle Jake doesn't want to hear me tell him that "There's a small chance I might die, Uncle. How's work going?"

The entire scene is, like, for real, literally a pity party. This is what people imagine when they make that analogy. I'm already in my old room an hour before my mother let my last cousin out. I'm not sleeping. God knows I can't do that, no matter how tired I feel. But I'm definitely in do not disturb mode. My door is closed and the lights are off. I think everyone got the hint.

I wake up the next morning to my parents' voices. Before that, I woke up sometime in the middle of the night to use the bathroom and saw my dad laying on the couch and staring at the ceiling. I knew they weren't about to sleep in the same room after Chloe dropped that bomb. But somehow, I feel like that wasn't the only reason my father's eyes were wide open.

"She's still not answering, Tommy." Solemn words from my mother snap me back to the moment. She's not even trying to whisper. I hear my dad mumble some kind of encouraging words then my mom picking up the house phone.

"Did you try texting her again?" My mom asks my dad this for the second time since I've been listening. She knows the answer.

"I'll do it again, Kay. She hasn't answered any of my messages yet, but I'll keep trying." My mom interrupts and they both end up saying 'keep trying' at the same time. I felt their fear through the walls. I stayed in bed another hour listening to their words turn more and more frantic. I tried to place my own feelings. Am I scared? Nope. That isn't it. A little sad but that isn't overwhelming, either.

I feel something, though. I'm not completely numb to what's happening. What that something is I couldn't tell. Then it hit me. Justin. Of course. I need to see Justin. No, I need to feel Justin. Once I finally got clear I realize that 'something' is hormones. It's been so long it almost feels new. I creep my fingers under my sheets, lifted my panties and shifted my legs.

A few short breaths and it's over. Never before has it happened that fast, but I still feel satisfied. When I walk into the living room, I'm dressed and my suitcase is packed.

"I'm ready to go now." Neither of my parents say a word. Dad looks at me then looks away. My mother just keeps staring.

"Your flight's not for another two days, Treasure." She sounds almost unsure.

"I know that, and I don't care. I'm ready to leave right now. There's no point in me staying here. The thought of staying another two days is making me sick." More blank stares.

Then my dad: "What if you stay one more day, Treasure? It will give us time to get a new flight and…"

"No. No, no, no. I'm not staying in this place another minute. My bags are packed and I'm ready to go right now. I don't care if I have to sit in the airport and wait all day for a flight. I'm getting out of here and I'm getting out of here today."

That's about all it takes. I don't even have to wait long for a standby. I can see Valleyfield below me now, smaller and smaller before it becomes invisible. Relief, contentment, maybe even a touch of pure joy all wrapped around me on that plane ride back to Toronto. Back to my home. Back to Justin. Life feels better already.

***

I'm really starting to hate hearing my phone ring. It freaks me out. Probably because I know it's my mom or dad, but partly because a phone call makes things seem so serious. I'm still good with texts. Nothing serious ever happens over text. A few breakups here and there with old flings, some finger wars when I'm pissed at Justin. But that's about it.

Calling someone implies so much more. Like a text won't do, we have to speak right now. The urgency is just different, and that's why my phone stays on silent now. Not even vibrate, straight silent mode.

I've made a decision. I don't give a fuck. Not about my sickness, not about my fake, real mother, not about returning any calls. I'm good, and I'm gonna be good until I'm not good anymore. That's it.

Justin's happy with me not giving a shit. It means he gets his girlfriend back. Back to how I was when we met in person. Yes, that girl. That Treasure. And I felt like I've made this declaration before, or something like it. But this time is real. This time I mean it. I'm only hoping that it's not too late for us. Me and Justin, Justin and I. I hope he's still here with me.

I'm a bit worried about that. I feel something I don't like. This hesitation. Pretending, even. Like he's trying to love me. Wow, that thought is hard to swallow. I hope I'm wrong. I hope that's just some female insecurity or failing female intuition. I just hope I'm wrong, but I know I'm not. Not completely. Either way, that's not stopping me from being crazy in love with him.

Nothing could do that, no one could make that happen. Except time, of course. When it stops my world. When it chooses to end my existence. All those ridiculous sayings won't mean a thing once time decides to take hold.

Better luck next time. There is no next time.

Tomorrow is another day. There is no tomorrow.

If at first you don't succeed, try and try again. Again is over.

Now how do you console someone? How do you convince them to believe in any of these concepts when they can see their end? It's strange because we all know we'll die eventually, but only those who are close to death start fearing it. Like seriously fearing it.

Or accepting it.

I'm somewhere in the middle. Depends what day of the week you catch me. Sometimes I think I'm more scared of the process of dying. The weakening, the lying in a bed in some hospital or some room wilting away while the ones who love you most try to hold back their own fear, their own disgust, their own insecurities.

Who thinks like this? Does anyone except me really think these thoughts? I know what my parents are thinking. My mom just can't deal right now. She's in full denial and will stay there till they close my casket. Dramatic, I know. It's not even inevitable. But I share my mother's fatalistic thinking disguised as optimism. The kind of optimism that says everything will be alright no matter the circumstances.

My birth story all over again.

Green as ancient emeralds.

One beauty mark, two beauty marks, three beauty marks...

Lies disguised as facts. Fiction disguised as memoire. Only the one telling the story knows the difference, knows the truth. Everyone else has only their perspective. And right now, Justin's perspective is all that matters.

"You gonna take all day in there?" Justin's hurrying me out of the bathroom again. It's Tuesday evening. Late enough in fall that all the leaves have fully turned, most of them piled in front of homes on the sidewalks. The rest are still falling. Every time we walk, I think I'm Dorothy. Except that our yellow brick road is covered in red and orange and gold leaves.

Justin has become a lion again, courage fully in tact. He plans dates on the most random days of the week. He never tells me where we're going, just whether or not I'll need to wear heels.

He takes my hand as soon as we leave the apartment and doesn't let go till we've arrive at whatever outing he's been planning for the week. Last week was cool. He took me to this kind of interpretive dance festival thing at the Sony Center. I'm pretty sure we were the youngest ones there. I did see another young couple and we all gave each other a little head nod.

The ballet companies were as magical as you'd expect. Seeing a dozen or more dancers maneuver across the stage, float almost, or sometimes they'd glide from one side to the next, all in unison, all effortless.

The composition that stood out the most to me wasn't ballet, though. At least not classic ballet. They were two dancers, a young man and a young woman. You can tell they were in love, but she had a history of failed relationships. Abusive relationships. She was scared.

He was ready. All he wanted was to be in love. To show her how special she was. And he tried. And he tried and he tried. And she tried, too. But how do you fight away your memories? Only time, right? If at first you don't succeed. Better luck next time and all that junk.

She fought, and he fought. But in the end, it wasn't enough. Love wasn't enough, not on its own. The routine ends in limbo. You actually don't know which way the story goes. I saw it as a tragedy, but when I spoke to Justin, he saw hope.

"If you told me where we were going, getting ready wouldn't take this long."

"If I told you where we were going, it would ruin all the fun."

"No, it wouldn't. It doesn't have to be a surprise to be fun."

"You need to stop talking and hurry up. We're gonna be late."

Even when he's annoyed he's still adorable. Tonight, he leaves the dress code open.

"Wear what you want," he says.

When I step out of the bathroom, he's not leaning against the front door with his shoes on waiting as I pictured he'd be. Instead he's sitting on one of our stools, shoes off, dressed more formally than he made me think was necessary.

"Do you know what day this is?"

I go through the list. Anniversary? No. His birthday? No. Valentine's day or something? Nope.

"Why don't you give me a hint?" I finally say. Justin laughs.

"This is the anniversary of the first day we met. The first day you stepped into this apartment."

Who is this guy? I don't even remember the first day we met. I mean, I remember what happened on that day, but not the exact date. I barely remembered the month. But this guy, he just keeps coming. I keep beating him over the head and he gets right back up and keeps on coming.

"I have gifts." He scurries over to the bedroom and pulls out a small box that he holds in one hand like he's delivering drinks at a fine dining restaurant. The first thing he takes out of the box is an empty plate.

"Because you never took a single line off this plate that night," he says.

Next came a solid gold necklace with an emerald pendant.

"Because the first thing I noticed were your eyes." He puts the box down and hooks the pendant around my neck. His fingers are warm but still make me shiver.

The last thing he pulled out of the box is a framed picture. Actually, it isn't a picture at all. It's my fake Facebook post about selling some of my makeup or something.

"Because this is the day I knew we'd be together forever. It's the day we found each other. No more dreaming."

I had no chance. I start sobbing, uncontrollably. Not cute crying with a few tears crawling down the side of my cheeks, I mean full out sobbing. I try covering my face. I'm in Justin's arms now. I'm planted in his chest. I can hear him saying *I love you, Treasure*. I can't say anything at the moment, but am not sure I would even if I wasn't temporarily incapacitated.

A knock on the door.

"Oh, by the way. I ordered pizza." Now I burst out laughing, just as ridiculously as I was wailing. *How does he do it?*

***

JUSTIN

I've been thinking about Treasure lately. The Treasure of my dreams. The girl I met when she was just a girl. It's hard not to reminisce about how we were then, about who we were. Thinking about it now, we really didn't even know each other. We were two dreamers in limbo, till the universe worked some kind of magic spell that brought us together.

Queen Street looks murky today. The roads, the sidewalks, all of it looks tinted and scummy. The clouds are just as dark. I'm sitting on my balcony where it's warm enough for a sweater but nothing less. People are moving slowly down Abell, up Lisgar, across Sudbury. Lisgar is a one way now, and a cruiser just sits parked in the post office lot pulling drivers over.

I need to get pulled over, I think to myself. Someone needs to ask me why the heck I'm going down this one way. I can see the cop pointing. She's telling the driver that just one street over and he can drive in the other direction. She'll probably just give the driver a warning and send them on their way.

No such luck for me, though. I'm headed the wrong way down a one way just waiting to crash head on. This is not me dreaming anymore. This is happening. Like, right now, happening.

"What are you gonna do, Justin?" I repeat that to myself over and over. "You have to do something." Of course, my parents come to mind. I wouldn't even have to ask them for help. I'd just watch them interact, listen to the way they speak to each other, and find the answer. That's how it worked with us. There were no special "talks." Neither of them ever sat me down to tell me what to expect or how to deal with a specific situation. All of the answers were right there. All I had to do was pay attention.

Like, there was never a problem with me going out when I was in high school. They knew I'd always be back home. They never gave me a curfew or anything. Not once. But I always came back at a reasonable time. If I was any later than I thought, I'd send my mom a text. The only reason I was like that was because that's how my parents were. My mom or dad wouldn't come stumbling inside at some crazy hour. They always let me know where they were going and texted me if they were going to be late.

It worked for our family. I was never really treated like a little kid. I had freedom, the freedom to do what I wanted. I pushed that freedom to its limits sometimes, but never went too far off the rail. But here I am now, teetering at the deep end. The cliff of a waterfall.

What am I really scared of? Like really, Justin, what are you scared of? I love this girl, right? I love this girl more than anything. And she loves me, too. We're good. We're more than good. We're actually doing great. Better than I'm making it out to be, at least. I don't even know why I'm stressing so hard.

"Fuck it." I say that out loud. I'm not about all this depression stuff, or this emotional ping pong. Treasure's alive right now, I need to be alive, too. My eyes are open. I start planning random dates again. Like really random. I just wake up, find out what's happening in the city that day, and go for it. Sometimes it's stuff I like, sometimes it's something I think Treasure might like, or sometimes it's just something new I want us to experience together.

Like one time, I got us tickets to the ballet. Don't ask me why. They had these discounted tickets online and I thought why not. It turned out to be one of our most amazing nights. Treasure wouldn't stop talking about it the whole streetcar ride back to our apartment.

Sometimes, we wouldn't go anywhere. I'd let Treasure get dressed up just so we could sit inside The Theatre Centre, or if it was a really nice day, we'd walk over to Trinity Park. One evening, I made her get semi dressed up just to give her a bunch of gifts and eat pizza. I told her it was the anniversary of the day we met. It wasn't the exact day, or even the month, to be honest. But I know Treasure doesn't remember those kind of things, so I took the risk. She didn't seem to mind. She was fine with it.

She was fine. She is fine. She really didn't care if we went to the park, or to a poetry slam at The Great Hall, or to a symphony. Treasure was always just happy to be with me. Did I forget? Like did I really forget this? I'm racking my brain trying to figure out when our relationship became all about me and my shit.

See, there I go again. I'm not even going through shit. Wait, that's not exactly true. I mean, yes, I did lose both my parents and I feel that loss everyday. It's like a virus that's infiltrated my bloodstream and is circulating throughout my entire body. I live with it, just like Treasure is living with her pain.

Wow! This is what Oprah would call an "aha" moment. Me and Treasure are so much more similar than I imagined, and that's saying a lot considering our history. I'm such an idiot. The biggest idiot. Whatever. At least I got here. At least she's smiling again. At least I'm out of this rut. Love...who would've known?

***

TREASURE

I feel like my parents are dying. I have this image of them back in Valleyfield sitting at opposite ends of the couch staring at the T.V with the volume off. I don't even know what's happening. I don't get daily calls anymore. Even when I do speak to my parents, it's never at the same time. It's like they're living in separate homes, and while I know it hasn't reached that point, I can sense their distance.

I know how I'm supposed to feel, but I don't. This isn't my fault. I know that as clearly as I know that I'm the cause. My parents have killed any updates to the situation with my birth mother, so I have no idea what's happening with all of that. Not that I'm really worried about it, or giving it much thought. It just sucks because I know they feel like so much of their life is out of their control.

That's a little BS, though. I mean, they could've just not had kids. They could've let my birth mother see me. My dad could've told my mom the truth. Not sure what the full story is there, but I know it's not roses.

I'm actually kind of curious to know what the deal is. Did my father cheat on my mother with my mother? My birth mother, I mean. And did he convince her to get pregnant because my mother couldn't? No way. I can't see how that's true. But then again, why would Chloe say those things if there wasn't something to it? And why wouldn't my father come right out and call her a liar if it wasn't true?

Can you see how crazy all of this is? How can you not lose your mind trying to make sense of any of it? So, I don't. I brush my hair. I put on a thong under my jeans to go to the grocery store. I smile at the guys who stare. Just a smile, then keep it moving. I'm a good girl now.

But where are my parents to see all of this? Why can't they realize that I'm happy? I don't need them sledge hammering their marriage trying to fix things. I hate that. I hate anyone feeling like they need to fix me. Of course, I want to be in the clear with this whole sickness, but it's not my life. Not even close. But it seems like it's everything to my parents.

Now they're suffering. Because of me, they're suffering. And even though I don't feel any guilt, I still hate it. I can see my mother floating right now. Floating through the house, floating through her classes, floating through making dinner. I can hear her students whispering at recess about how something is wrong with Mrs. Zahariah.

"She doesn't look the same anymore."

"I heard her daughter is dying."

"I heard her husband has another baby."

Whispers, whispers, whispers. Small town whispers turn molehills into mountains. Don't I know it. I lived it. My mom has been living it. Wait, my mom *has* been living it. Has she? How long has she been dealing with these whispers? I was so caught up in my own longing to leave Valleyfield, in my own feelings, my own dreams, that I never thought that my mother ever had to deal with anything.

But she must have been hearing these whispers since the day I was born. She must have walked into rooms that would go silent. She must have felt gazes a second too long or endured looks from men with degrading thoughts, maybe even degrading words. How did she do it? Why would she do it? Why wouldn't she just leave?

I can't believe I've never thought about this before. I'm such an idiot. A selfish idiot.

"Hey, Mommy." I couldn't help myself.

"Hello, dear. Is something wrong?" Phone calls are alarming even when I'm the one making the call.

"No, nothing is wrong. Just called to say hi." Silence. "And that I want to try. I want to try calling her." Still no reaction.

"I think it'll make a difference if she hears my voice on her voicemail."

"I think so, too, Treasure." My mom didn't even ask me if this would be too much. She didn't ask if I'm sure or try to convince me that I didn't have to do this. She let it go. I took it and she let me.

But now I have it. Now I'm the one who has to make this work. I'm fighting percentages. My illness isn't terminal but my parents' marriage will be if I don't at least make this effort. Don't ask me how I know that. Don't ask me how I know that I'm fighting a disease that is contagious. Not actually, but it might as well be. A strange kind of contagious that infects only the ones closest to you. Only the ones you love the most.

And they don't die. Not physically. But their lives are ruined all the same. Their bonds are broken, relationships fractured, careers put on hold. Everything is different. My parents are infected, so I have to do this. I have to.

Not on my own, though. I need Justin with me. I've left him out of too many of these instances. Not this time. This time I'll make sure he's right beside me every time I dial her number, or send a text or an email, or even answer her calls. He's always been here, through it all, and I'm done trying to keep him away.

I'll do it on my own time though. I'll put it off as long as I can. It's almost a week before I even tell Justin about the conversation with my mom. Surprise, surprise; he's ready to be supportive.

"I'm down, baby. Whatever you need." Of course. But what I need now are a few more days of not thinking about this. A few more days of calm before shit gets real. But it's no use. The tension is in every conversation, every walk to the convenience store, every second I stand in the express line at FreshCo waiting to cash out.

So, it's time to suck it up. It's time to pull up my skirt and make this thing happen. My cell phone and a glass of white. Justin and the couch. Let's just get this over with.

***

I'm not sure I want to do this anymore. What the fuck was I thinking? I'm definitely not doing this. I can't. My parents just need to get over it. They need to deal with whatever issues they have on their own. Don't make me the problem, because I'm not. They're the problem. They're the ones who need help. Not me. I'm good. I've always been good.

Why should I have to go through this? My doctor said a million times that I'm fine for now. Yes, there's a chance that something might happen. Yes, the only way to forever keep me in the clear is through this allogeneic transplant. But until that day comes, why are we even thinking about this?

The city looks tragic today. It's been more than a week and parts of the sidewalks are still blocked off by small fences and yellow tape. Something's up with the streetcars because now I see buses marked 501. When it rains, we hear every drop from inside of our apartment. It's like fake fingernails tapping against a metal desk.

It's hard not to reminisce on these days. I let my mind wander not on my own memories, but on some of the stories Justin has told me. I don't think he notices how similar we are. I mean he does, but he doesn't. Not like how I notice.

When he told me stories of his high school days, I'd just shake my head.

"You were the male version of me," I'd tell him.

"More like you were the female version of me."

Hearing about all his adventures with different girls, his friendship with Steve, even being a single child and getting all the attention from both parents. All of it was so similar. Then for him to lose all of that. I couldn't even deal, and neither can Justin, really. He still struggles with it, as he should.

The thought of losing both my parents is so far out of this world for me. Not that I call them everyday or visit them as much as I should, but I can. And that's what Justin reminds me. *You can still do all of those things,* he says. *You can take your parents for granted as long as you want, till you can't. My parents did so much for me and I felt like I did nothing for them. So, if you have a chance to do something now that would make a difference in their lives, why not do it.*

Can't say I saw that coming, but I really should stop being surprised by this guy. Justin knows me, and it was the push I needed at the time I needed it. I couldn't leave my parents hanging like this. Not when it means so much to them. And really, it's me who they're worried about. It's my circumstances that's stressing them out and causing whatever breech is poisoning their marriage. Dialing a few numbers is the least I can do.

So, I do it. I actually do it. I close my eyes and press send.

***

JUSTIN

Panic. That's the last thing I remember. Now I'm dreaming, but this isn't the same world. Treasure's not here. At least I don't see her. I want to but I can't. I feel myself searching my mind, creating spaces I think she'll appear, building memories she should occupy. But nothing. Nothing.

This world isn't my world. I need to get out. Panic. Lights and more lights. Sounds I don't recognize, scenes I've never seen, this isn't my world.

"Treasure!"

The lights keep getting brighter. She's still not here. She's still not answering. I'm running. Away from the lights. Away from all of those lights.

"Treasure!"

The lights are chasing me now. The faster I run, the closer it gets. I can hear Steve now. He's telling me not to stop running. Not to give up. *Why would I give up? Why is he here? This is not his world.* This is not my world. I need to get out. I need Treasure. Where the fuck is Treasure?

It's quiet now. The lights have all dimmed but I still hear the sounds. Steady. Faint. Quiet. I'm still in this world I don't recognize, this dream that makes no sense. This dream where time makes no sense. I don't know how long it's been. I try opening my eyes. I try but it's not working, my eyes are not working.

More panicking. I need to catch my breath. *Calm down, Justin. Calm the fuck down and think. What's the last thing you remember? Where were you? Who were you with?* I'm pressing my eyes closed. Deep breaths. Long, deep breaths. Still nothing. It's no use. I'm not even panicking any more. It's way past that now. Now I'm just scared.

I think about my parents. They feel close. My eyes are open but I'm not sure what I'm seeing. I can make out voices more clearly than I can objects or people. One by one, I hear different conversations. Then I hear her. Treasure. She's speaking through tears. I can tell because her voice changes when she's crying, each word like a different key on a piano.

She's saying something. "It's my fault." It doesn't make sense. What's her fault, and why is she crying? Why can't I see her? *"Treasure!"* Why isn't she answering? I'm screaming now, loud as I can. *"Treasure!"* Nothing. More slurred apologies, more explanations, more sobbing. It's starting to make sense.

***

TREASURE

There was this thing we used to do with the BAGS. We started it when we were still running the group out of the church. We'd let the kids go one by one into the confessional on their own. No one else there listening, just them. We'd tell them that for three minutes they could say whatever they wanted. They didn't have to tell me or Amanda what they said, but they had to say something and they had to stay in there the full three minutes.

We called it paradise. The kids loved it.

"When can we go to paradise, Treasure?"

"Can I go to paradise first today, Amanda?"

Who knows what they said inside that booth? Sometimes, we'd hear a muffled scream and get a bit nervous. But we knew they were just getting it all out. They needed that. Somewhere to get all their shit out without feeling judged, without feeling guilty, without having to apologize. Holding too much stuff in is dangerous. It's dangerous because you never know when or how it's going to come out.

And people are wrong to think that the danger is building up to some big explosion. That's not it. What's more common are the small outbursts of frustration. It's those days where little things bother you more than they should, and you can't figure out why you're this upset when it really isn't that big of a deal. You snap at a friend for no reason. You lay in bed for hours, half watching the TV, half dazed out in your own world. By the time the explosion comes, it's already too late.

Justin has just exploded, and I missed all his little outbursts before this. He was screaming as loudly as my BAGS in paradise with no one there to hear him. It was so obvious. He was right in front of me. Everyday, he was right in front of me and I didn't see it. I didn't see him. And now...

One thing I did notice since we first hooked up is that Justin doesn't want things; Justin needs things. It was one of his traits that made me feel so special. He never made me feel like his life could go on without me. He needed me in it as much as he needed his blood to flow or his heart to beat. Then our hearts started beating together and that was that. Twin souls.

I remember Justin telling me about how his parents met. He said his mom was already engaged to someone else. She was only two months away from getting married when she met his dad.

"She was working at the AGO and he just strolled in by himself one morning. My mom was working one of the new exhibitions when she saw him. She said as soon as he said hi, she knew right away."

He followed her around the gallery for the rest of the day. The next week, she broke off her engagement. A year later, Justin was born. These things happen fast, and if you're not ready, it can pass you by. I always felt two ways about that story. First, it made me realize that Justin's impulsiveness is hereditary. Funny, yes, but it gave me some perspective. What was more important was that it made me believe even more in fate. It made me believe that trusting my gut was that important. There was magic happening all around me and Justin long before we were ever dreaming, long before we ever met, long before we were ever here.

Now here we are. I'm not even freaking out right now. I'm not. I got this. There's no way the universe works this hard to bring two people together to have it end like this. There's more to this story. There's more to me and Justin; I'm sure of it. He's all that matters right now. All that other stuff can wait.

***

JUSTIN

I'm starting to see now. I didn't at first, but now I'm starting to see. Actually, it's more like I'm starting to understand. I'm lost. I'm not sure how I got here, but I know I'm lost. I've been wandering for what must be days, maybe weeks, maybe longer. There's no way to tell in this world. There's no day and night, there's no sunrise or sunsets, there is no sleep. I'm lost, and what's worse is that I'm alone.

I see glimpses of my life. Sometimes I just hear. I'm fighting, though. That much I know. I know because there's no way I don't get to see Treasure again. There's no way I don't get to wake up to Treasure every morning. Not without at least saying goodbye. The universe doesn't work this hard to bring two people together just to have it end like this. No way.

Treasure. She must be so fucking pissed right now. I picture her calling in sick to work, not answering any phone calls, searching for a way to find me. I can't help but smile.

"This girl," I think to myself. "Only this girl."

Things are starting to clear up now. I'm remembering. Lines and lines and lines on a plate. Pills and tequila. Tame Impala and Nirvana. Now the doctors' voices are more precise. They're asking if it's accidental or intentional. I'm asking myself the same thing. Why would I do this? Did I mean to do this?

But then I think. I don't believe in accidents. How can I believe in accidents? Everything in my life has been fate working its treacherous magic. Fate killed my parents on the same day it struck my girlfriend. Fate made me dream. Fate made my dreams come true. How can I not believe that it's these same forces at work that brought me here?

I need to focus, though, because I'm not staying here. I'm not getting stuck in this limbo wandering for the rest of my life. I have a life, a real one, and it's waiting for me. She's waiting for me. I hear her telling the doctors she's not leaving without me. That they can do whatever they need to do, but she's not walking out of that hospital unless I'm walking with her.

"You're my treasure," she's talking to me now. "You've always been my treasure, Justin. Fight. Fight for the both of us. There's no me without you, Justin. You fight for the both of us."

It's still hazy. I'm still stuck in my mind. I'm still trying to remember why I'm here. Panic. Yes, that's it. Drugs and liquor and panic. But why? How did I get so lost? I was supposed to be strong. This isn't like me. To just give in like that. To give up. Treasure must be so pissed. Steve must be scared out of his mind. I'm sure he's told my grandparents. Nothing's making sense. My thoughts all feel jumbled now, like they're circling in a washing machine trying to get clean.

I know what I have to do.

***

TREASURE

I can still remember my very first day in Toronto. I was just as anxious as I was excited. I was also trying not to be too pissed off about my mom and dad dropping that bomb on me the day before I left. Can you imagine trying to deal with that right before leaving your home for the first time? Right before being alone in a new place, a far away place.

I remember my first day because I didn't do anything. All that talk about starting a new life and being this whole new person and on my first day in this new city, I do nothing. How's that for irony? I blamed it on jet lag. I blamed it on not having anyone to show me where to go. Truth is, I just didn't want to do anything.

Truth is, I didn't come to this city to be this party girl. I didn't come here to "find myself" or anything like that. I'm here because I'm supposed to be here. Something was pushing me out of Valleyfield and pointing me to this city. Then by some weird stroke of fate, I met that something. The universe made it clear the day I met Justin that he was my reason for coming here.

My parents ask me about how he's doing. "The same," I tell them. "Still alive so that's all that matters, but he hasn't come out of his coma yet." They ask me how I'm doing. They want to know if I need them to fly down. If their being here would help.

"I'm not the one you need to worry about. I'll be fine. Justin's laying in a hospital bed so unless you have some kind of elixir that's gonna change that, then you might as well stay in Valleyfield."

They linger on the phone. They want to know more. They want to know how the call went and if I was able to convince Chloe to finally change her mind. I don't even give them the chance.

"Don't even bother, Mom. This is just not the right time."

"Not the right time? Do you even know what you're saying? You have an illness that requires monthly treatments. You have an illness that can get worse at any time and end your life. Justin being in a coma doesn't change that. If there's something we can do now to make things better, then we need to do it. You can't just push it to the side like if his life matters more than yours."

"His life does matter."

"I don't care about his life, Treasure. I care about you. I care about your life. My daughter. *My* daughter. And I'm not going to leave this up for chance because you're infatuated with some boy."

The thing that sucks about smart phones is that you can't slam them when you're upset. Simply pressing end doesn't let the person on the other end of the phone know how upset you are, but it's all I could do. And I get it. I know what my mom's going through. She just wants me to get better, but I just want Justin to wake up. At least my mom can still yell at me and make me feel like a five-year-old who got in trouble at school for pulling another girl's hair. Justin can't even open his eyes.

But I can close mine. I can close my eyes and find him. Search my dreams until he appears. We've done it before when we were hundreds of miles apart. Now we're close. Now we're connected on a level no one can possibly understand. It's been just two days and already I can't stand myself without Justin here with me. I need him. I need to feel him touching my beauty marks. I need him carrying me on his back. He's the only one. He is the only one.

***

JUSTIN

I was beside her when she made that call. I remember that. She left the phone on speaker so I could be part of the conversation, even though we both knew I wouldn't be saying a word. Treasure sat with her legs crossed at the head of the bed. She spun the ring on her index finger, pulled at the bands on her wrists, even tried to crack her knuckles a few times. I was on my stomach with my chin perched on Treasure's leg when the phone started ringing.

"She's not gonna answer," Treasure said. "She just won't." And she didn't.

"Leave a message," I tell Treasure, who finally let her eyes open when the phone rang for the last time.

"No, I'll just call back."

"No, you won't, Treasure. Leave the message right now." I said that almost simultaneously with the sound of the beep. I got ready for Treasure to mumble some words into the phone, but she pulled herself together and left a coherent voicemail asking Chloe to call her back. And she did.

It's strange how blood can tie two strangers together. Treasure and Chloe have no shared memories. They've only seen each other three times in both their lives: when Chloe gave birth to Treasure, the night of the accident, and when Treasure and her family arranged that meeting in Valleyfield a short time ago. But you can have your ear to the wall in another room eavesdropping on their conversation and tell they were connected in some way.

Their voices sound identical. The way they change their tone to make a point was identical. I'm almost sure Chloe was probably sitting at home crossed legged in her bed twiddling her fingers just as Treasure was at that moment they first spoke.

"I really don't know what I'm asking for," Treasure said. "I mean, I know what I need, and know what my parents would love to happen, but I really don't know what I want from you."

I gave Treasure one of those confused looks. I couldn't figure out what she was saying. Of course, she knew what she wanted. She wanted Chloe to go through with the procedure. That was the whole point of the phone call. That was what Treasure needed to get fully healthy. I really didn't get it.

Chloe must have been just as curved because she didn't say anything for a few seconds.

"You gave birth to me, right? You carried me for nine months, did everything during that time to make sure I was healthy, then pushed me out. Then just like that, you were gone. You didn't even have the choice to be part of my life. I can't imagine what that must've felt like for all these years."

"Painful." It's the only word Chloe could muster through her sniffles. Surprisingly, Treasure's eyes were still dry. Her hands had stopped fidgeting and she sat almost motionless on our bed. It's like something had gotten into her, like deep enough inside to give her this manufactured strength.

"I'm giving you a choice now. You can be in my life even if you choose not to go through with this whole thing. And I mean that. I know my parents are all worked up about this procedure, but I'm fine right now. I take the medication I need to take, go to all my monthly sessions, and I'm living a good life. You can be part of that. You should be part of that."

That's it. That's my last memory of Treasure. The last time I consciously heard her voice, or played with her hair, or counted her beauty marks. The last time I remember sharing a moment with the girl of my dreams. Now I can't escape my dreams, or I should say this nightmare that's taken over my life. It all feels so impossible.

I lied before. I really don't know what I have to do. I'm just as lost now as I was when I first realized I was in this world. Time still feels absent, the days and nights and minutes and hours all feel irrelevant here. There's nothing left.

***

TREASURE

You ever believe in something too incredible to make any sense? Like a single God watching over us, guiding us, a creator whose children are every living thing on this earth? Or maybe like aliens that are somewhere off in a distant galaxy with technology that's light years ahead of anything we have on our own planet.

I think love is that incredible, or at least it can be. I know it's the most powerful force we all have the potential to tap into without having to be geniuses. It's already in us, in all of us, we just need triggers to bring it out. Justin is definitely my trigger.

He doesn't even need to do anything to set me off. Except overdose and end up in a hospital stuck in a coma for who knows how long. It's the third night I fall asleep angled on this steel chair beside Justin's bed. It scares me, closing my eyes, so I fight it. I pace the room as long as my legs can bare, sit in awkward positions that should be impossible to pass out, and load up on hospital coffee that at this point might as well be from Mabel's.

I'm exhausted, but it's better than the alternative. I don't want to wake up to Justin still sleeping. I have these vivid images in my mind of opening my eyes to a bunch of doctors trying desperately to revive Justin with the nurse screaming at me to wait outside. Shonda Rhimes would be proud at my imagination, but those thoughts frightened me enough to set an alarm on my phone timed for every hour.

But this night is different. This night, I welcome sleep. This night, I look forward to the images that will appear once I let myself doze off. It could be my only chance. My only chance to speak with him again, to have him look at me like no one else ever has. We met in our dreams, fell in love through our minds, so why can't love bring us back together?

Somehow, I knew Justin was thinking the same thing. He was calling for me, screaming for me to show up. I get it now. I hear him. I know what I need to do. The only thing is how do I control it? How do I make myself dream of Justin? All those other times were random. We didn't have to convince ourselves to see each other; it just happened. We just happened. Now I need to make this happen, and I need to make it happen tonight.

The longer Justin stays in this coma, the less likely he is to ever get out of it. I can't deal with that. I've already made up my mind that he's not leaving me like this. So tonight, this night, shit's about to change.

One by one, I pass each of my fingers across his lips.

"I'm coming," I say it so only he can hear even though no one else is in the room.

"Till we dream again, right? I'm gonna dream till I see you, Justin. Till we're back together like we're supposed to be, like we're meant to be."

"He can't hear you."

I guess I was wrong. Steve is standing at the inside of the room door with his hands folded behind his back.

"He's in a coma. You realize that, right? It means he's not conscious."

I try my best not to sound like I want to rip his head off and feed it to his dog.

"I know he's in a coma. That doesn't mean he can't hear what I'm saying. Maybe you should try talking to him, unless you have some more excuses for not being around." Zero patience.

"Me not being around? That's hilarious. Because I was thinking that if you weren't around so much, he wouldn't be in a coma in the first place."

Is this guy insane? What the heck is he talking about? How on earth could it be my fault that Justin's in the hospital? Steve doesn't even give me a chance to respond.

"All he thinks about is you. All he stresses about is you. Treasure, Treasure, Treasure. And for what? You're barely worth the nights we spent together. You never loved him an ounce as much as he loved you."

Steve is getting closer as he's firing off these insults. I'm still sitting at Justin's bedside.

"I love Justin more than anything in my life. And he's still here so stop talking about him like he's gone. He's not going anywhere and neither am I."

"I know you aren't. That's the problem. You need to get out of his life. You don't know how to appreciate him. You don't even know how to be faithful. Running around with that Samantha girl. Oh, sorry, I mean that woman. Justin told me all about that."

I can feel the heat in my neck. I turn my head away from Steve. My only thought right now is not to disturb Justin, not to let him feel this animosity around him.

"Then you kiss me."

"What? I never touched you, you fucking creep! *You* kissed *me*."

"And you let me."

"I got away from you."

"Not before you kissed me back. Just admit it, Treasure, you can't be with just one person. That's not who you are. There's not enough excitement in being monogamous, so why don't you just take this opportunity to get out of Justin's life. If he wakes up, I'll tell him you said bye."

Now I'm wondering what the punishment is for stabbing someone in the heart. Probably light, considering Steve doesn't have one. He's right in front of me now. I haven't moved since he started this tangent.

"When are you gonna get over me?" I say this without any tremble in my voice. "Like really, when are you going to get it through your skull that you were just a pastime? I didn't care about you, Steve. You were fun for minute, then you weren't. So, do me a favour, when you're done throwing your little tantrum, maybe you should go find a roof to fall over. I'm sure you won't be missed."

When Justin gets better, we're really going to have to do something about this guy. He'll never stop. He'll never get over the fact that I chose his best friend over him. He thinks he lost out on something special when in reality we never had anything special. Like not even close.

I can tell that he wants to say more. He's searching for a comeback that will sting at least half as much as my words hurt him. But I know that look. I know his type. He's got nothing, so he says something about me being a slut and walks out the door. What a good friend.

I don't even have time to be mad at Steve. Justin still hasn't moved, still hasn't said a word, he still needs me, and I still need him. Tonight, we dream. Tonight, we find each other again and heal our scars.

***

JUSTIN

The memories are getting painful now. No wonder I blanked them out. The more I remember about how I ended up down here, the less I want to know, or want to believe. Now I remember Steve telling me something about Treasure. Something she did, or he did, or they did together.

"There's no way," I told him. "I don't believe you."

"Believe it, buddy. It happened right by the door."

I shook my head. I asked him why he would make up such a bullshit story.

"Why is it so hard to believe?" he asked me. "She's never been faithful to you. Just because Samantha's a girl doesn't mean it doesn't count. It's in her DNA. Pretty girls think they can get away with anything. You know that. You're just a bit head over heels right now so you can't see it."

Had I really been that blind? No, it's impossible. Treasure loves me. She loves me more than anything. I know that. So, what if she does whatever she does with Samantha? It's not the same as actually cheating. It just isn't. But that kiss, though. She wouldn't do that. Treasure would never hurt me like that. She hates Steve so I really don't get it.

I wish I could shut off my mind. Like flip a switch in my ear that makes all these thoughts just stop. I'm just tired. So damn tired. But how do you sleep when you're stuck in limbo? How do you close your eyes when you haven't opened them for who knows how long? There's nothing left for me. Nothing left but this. I think I'm finally letting that sink in.

"You again." That voice sounds too familiar, but it doesn't sound like the other voices. I can hear this voice as clear as I can hear my own thoughts.

"You didn't think I was gonna leave you in this place all by yourself, did you?"

I'm back on a bench near the lake. I'm back drawing shapes in the sand. Treasure's back behind me but this time she knows. She knows it's me. I turn around and I know it's her. I don't even wonder how this is possible. I don't even think to ask how this is happening. Treasure runs to me and jumps on my back. Her face is on my face, her lips move down my neck.

"You have to live," she says. "I want you to say it. Tell me you're gonna live." I turn and sit her down gently. We're settled in the sand with both my hands folded around hers.

"I'm gonna live, Treasure."

"No. I want you to say it and I want you to mean it. Tell me you're gonna live, Justin. Tell me that we're both gonna open our eyes and be back inside the hospital hand in hand. Tell me now."

I finally feel my eyes close. Treasure's energy surrounds us both. I can still see her staring right at me. She's telling me to live. She's telling me to open my eyes. I tell her I see her beauty marks. They're floating like soap bubbles through the sky.

"Beautiful," I say. "Beautiful."

***

TREASURE

Chloe can't help herself. She'll sit and search my face for what seems like minutes at a time without saying a word.

"Stop that," I tell her. She thinks I'm joking, and I am for the most part. But it does feel a bit awkward having someone stare at you, no matter who's the culprit. We're sitting at the corner couch in The Theatre Centre, the seats right by the window facing my street. Every passerby steals my attention and gives Chloe more chances for her visual inspections.

It's her second time in the city and she still can't figure out why there's a Starbucks on every other corner. Or why all the signage on the tops or sidewalks of restaurants promote vegan eating. "Vegan roti options," "baby steps are for babies, be vegan," "vegan is not a diet." She shakes her head every time she passes another one.

It's all amusing to Chloe. She walks light like she's lakeside in Muskoka in early August. Nothing is alarming, nothing is too hectic, no homeless person too much of a bother. She's been here for a week and is staying for one more, and I have to say that it's been one of the most peaceful stretches of the past few months.

Her first visit only lasted about six days. I remember seeing her stroll out from Billy Bishop airport and thinking that this was the first time I'd ever seen her walk. She rolled a beige carry-on paired with an oversized handbag resting on her other shoulder, nearly the same colour and covered in large print. I laughed because she almost looked stylish, like if she knew exactly how to fit into the city despite never setting foot here till that morning.

We'd spoken every day for a month before she finally got here. We talked more like sisters than anything else. Maybe not quite sisters, maybe like best friends who haven't seen or spoken to each other since high school. And just like best friends, it's like we hadn't missed a beat. It's like we forgot that we were actually strangers. That my parents hated her and hated me speaking to her about anything other than that thing that we should be talking about.

I really didn't care, though. After the first time I called Chloe, I knew what I wanted. I wasn't about to treat her like a product. I just wanted her to be in my life, or at least give her the choice of being in my life. That was never an option for her, and I don't see how that makes sense seeing how I wouldn't even be alive if it wasn't for her.

My parents got over it, though. Once they realized that I wasn't planning on not speaking to Chloe anytime soon, they got with it pretty quickly. I'm sure at first, they were just placating.

"It's great that you two are building a relationship, Treasure." I swear I could hear my mother clenching her teeth as she said those words. My dad never said anything about it, not to me, anyways. But he must have felt like he was skiing downhill with no flat land in sight. What's scarier is that he probably had no idea whether he was speeding towards my mom or away from her, and Chloe just made the trail that much steeper.

I left all that alone for now. I was watching an episode of The Good Fight on Netflix when one of the main characters spoke some real truth. Her name on the show is Diane and she's like a big shot lawyer. She's speaking to her goddaughter, who just passed the bar, and tells her that in law, you never trust your instincts. You sit back, wait, and listen, and eventually everyone will reveal themselves. Something like that.

I don't know about the not trusting your instincts part, but I think in this situation with my parents and Chloe, Diane's words have some merit. They may even turn out to be prophetic. Time. It's crazy how something we have no control over essentially controls our lives.

But by the time I got to talking to Chloe, I was fed up with being controlled. I wasn't about to let anything or anyone dictate my decisions except me. So, we didn't just talk on the phone, we FaceTimed. It was my idea, of course. I even made Chloe get an iPhone so we could make it happen. I knew she'd be game because it meant she got to see me all the time, but really, I was the one who wanted to see her.

I wanted to see her face. I wanted to see the way her arms moved pushing away her dog when he jumped on her couch during one of our calls, or the way she played with her bangs whenever she was thinking about what to say next. It mattered. Every body part, every blink, every turn of her head, it all mattered. So, by the time we met in person at the airport, we were already familiar. We were already family.

I can say that now without feeling like some kind of backstabber. And the truth of the matter is that Chloe was always family, so I should never have felt any guilt for feeling that way. Just like I never felt any guilt when Chloe actually agreed to go along with the procedure. And agreed is the wrong word because I never once asked her to do it. She got there, herself. She made that decision.

That was the reason for her first visit, and after we got through it, she rested at my apartment. Our apartment, I should say, mine and Justin's of course. That will never change whether Justin is here or not. And he will be back here, that much we know. And I can't wait till he's back counting my beauty marks every morning.

Chloe couldn't wait for the morning to get started. She was up before the apartment was lit, first just reading a book by Nino Ricci, who she said was her favourite author, then once some light finally squeezed through the windows, she'd be scrambling eggs or flour, or boiling water on the stove.

"I hate sleeping," she said. "If I never had to sleep another hour in my life, I wouldn't."

"Sleep is what changed my life," I told her, but wasn't quite ready to get into the whole Justin story. She knew enough, including him having been in that coma for nearly three days. She didn't pry. I guess she watched Netflix, too.

Although Chloe's first visit was more important to my life, her second visit is much more special. It's hard to put into words exactly what having Chloe around does for me. It's not like I missed her growing up. How could I? But now having her here, listening to her speak, watching her put her hair in a bun before she makes dinner, I almost feel like I've been robbed of something for all these years.

"I'm happy you're not a vegan," she says playfully. "You'd be on your own for dinner."

"Really? You ready to leave me alone already, huh?"

"Ha. Not a chance, my dear. You're stuck with me for life so good luck."

I take a deep breath. I've been waiting to ask Chloe this question face to face since the day we sat across from each other at the diner in Valleyfield. I pussied out a few times, but wasn't about to let her leave again without knowing.

"Growing up, my mom always told me this ridiculous story about how I was born in the back of my dad's truck. I pretty much knew it was bullshit, but it sounded cool, so I went with it. I want you to tell me how I was really born. Like what happened that day, for real."

At this point, I could pick up the spoon Chloe was using to mix lentil soup and stir the anxiety. It's the first time it ever feels there is a space between us. Chloe keeps stirring the pot and looks at me like I'd just asked her to buy me a Christmas gift she knew she couldn't afford.

"I think maybe you should let your parents tell you about that. I'm not sure it's really my place."

"How can it not be your place? I'm asking you. I'm the one that was lied to for most of my life so I think I deserve to hear it from all sides, wouldn't you say?"

I'm not sure how that sounded out of my mouth, but regardless, I apologize to Chloe for being pushy.

"I just wanna know the truth. It's not really a big deal, but it kind of is a big deal, if that makes any sense."

"It does, and of course knowing how you were born is a big deal." Chloe turns down the pot and moves around the kitchen counter to join me on the barstools.

"I don't think I can beat the backseat birth story, but I'll tell you the truth. The truth is, Kay wasn't there when you were born. Only your father was."

I opened my mouth to say something. "Bullshit" was the first word that came to mind. But I held it together and let Chloe finish. I asked for this.

"She was in the hospital, just not in the actual room. I don't think she wanted to see you coming out of me. It would've made everything too real. And seeing is believing, right. So, I guess she figured if she didn't see, then..."

"Then what? Then she wouldn't have to believe that you actually gave birth to me and she didn't."

"I'm not saying that's what she thought, Treasure, I'm only assuming. You have to remember that your father wasn't just sitting in a corner in the delivery room. He was holding my hand. He was keeping me calm. No woman, no matter what, wants to see her husband comfort another woman. It was a difficult situation for everyone, but something magical came from it. And for that, I'd do it all over again."

I don't know why I suddenly felt that I had on way too much clothes, or that I had to close my eyes to catch my breath. This was like the hangover from a night of Hennessey. Luckily, for once, Chloe wasn't searching me. She knew what she said and knew how I was taking it. Once I got over my silent meltdown, I needed to know more.

"So, were you and my dad a thing? Did you guys have...something?"

"That part is certainly not my place, Treasure. I will say that me and your father weren't strangers, but I'll leave it at that. I'm sure he'll get around to telling you everything soon enough."

Fair. But there's still one more thing I have to know.

"Treasure? Who came up with that name?" Chloe breaks out in a full hyena laugh and almost tumbles off the stool.

"That definitely wasn't me. Your dad was actually the one to name you. He said that no matter what else he did in his life, he wanted to treasure that moment forever. So, he named you Treasure as his way of never forgetting."

What could I say after that? Like, really, what is there to say? Chloe and I sit and hug and cry and laugh all in a single moment. Then we say forget about soup and order a box of King Slice and eat double chocolate brownies till the pizza arrives.

We don't sleep a wink on Chloe's last night. We don't do much of anything else, either. The TV is like background noise at a cafe, and we're both sitting with our feet up on the couch, lost in our own thoughts.

"When is Justin coming home?" Chloe finally breaks the silence.

"He has about three weeks left till he's allowed to come out. Feels like forever, though. But I just want him to be good, so it's well worth the wait."

"It's so amazing to find someone like that. You two must be so happy together."

"We are. He's everything, and I'm his everything. Like twin souls, if that makes sense."

"Twin souls? I like that. Sounds magical. I've had a few, um, encounters, myself, but I don't think I've ever experienced someone that's connected to my soul. Not like what you and Justin have."

I don't think anyone in the world has what me and Justin have. And what I love is that we both know how special we are together. We know we're a fluke, some kind of glitch in the universe that completely goes against any known or accepted order. We know it and that's why we're here. That's why we fight for each other, in this reality or any other realm of possibility.

I used to think I became beautiful by accident. Not anymore. Not by a long shot. I was spared physical scars to endure something much deeper, much more powerful, much more meaningful. I thought I didn't deserve any of this, but I was wrong. So wrong. This is my life. My dreams, Justin, my parents, Chloe, even Samantha, this was all made for me.

Till we dream again...

Acknowledgements

There are always so many people to thank for helping to put together something of this magnitude. From the random people I've observed up and down Queen street that piece together my characters, to my editor, Talia, who made profound edits seem rudimentary.

However, I wouldn't have found the confidence to take the chances I did in telling this story if it wasn't for my writing group. The Circle, as we call it, is about storytelling in its rawest form. The individuals who make up this group are all superior storytellers in their own right. Sitting with them for over two years, listening as they read their own tales and perspectives, inspired me to push outside of my own comfort zone and into the clouds of my imagination. For that, I thank you all dearly.